# NEW AGE SHORT STORIES

TO BRAD &
SHERRY —
WITH LOTS OF
LOVE & HUGS —

RICHARD SOTPAKE

# NEW AGE SHORT STORIES

## A COLLECTION
## DICK SUTPHEN

**Also By Dick Sutphen**

*From Pocket Books*
You Were Born Again to Be Together • Past Lives, Future Loves
Unseen Influences • Finding Your Answers Within
Earthly Purpose • The Oracle Within

*From Valley of the Sun*
Master of Life Manual • Enlightenment Transcripts
Lighting The Light Within • Past Life Therapy In Action
SEDONA: Psychic Energy Vortexes • Predestined Love
Heart Magic • Reinventing Yourself • Simple Solutions
The Spiritual Path Guidebook • Radical Spirituality

Copyrights © by Dick Sutphen, Malibu, CA, 1997. Some of the
stories were originally published elsewhere. "Ultra-Depth" first ran in
*Soaring Spirit* #60 – spring 1995. "Childhood Hero" and "The Woman
Who Visited Psychics" were part of the *Beneath Sedona* audio collection,
1990. A revised version of *The Lightbearer* was originally an audio book
on cassette, 1990. The other stories in the collection are new. All rights
reserved. No part of this book may be reproduced in any form without
written permission from the publisher, except for brief passages included
in a review. Art direction: Jason D. McKean. Printed in USA.

**Valley of the Sun Publishing, Box 38, Malibu CA 90265**

First Edition: October 1997

ISBN Number 0-87554-608-0
Library of Congress Card Number 97-61408

This book is lovingly
dedicated to the team:
my wife Tara,
Steve, Jason, Jessi,
Jan, Laura, Kim,
William & Travis

# Contents

# Ultra-Depth

In order to be considered as an ultra-depth hypnosis test subject, Jamie had to lie about being married. She needed money, and the $35 per session Dr. MacIntyre offered volunteers sure beat five hours waitressing at the Campus Cafe. So she did—even though she didn't know exactly what the testing entailed.

"Jamie Hamlyn, 32, divorced," the crew-cut, young male interviewer read from her application. "You attend school mornings, work as a data processor afternoons. No boyfriend, right?"

She shook her head. "Is that important?"

"Doctor Mac wants unattached subjects." He scanned the rest of the form. "If accepted after testing, you'll be asked to participate Tuesdays and Thursdays, 7 to 10 PM for eight weeks." He looked up to catch her reaction.

Jamie nodded, brushed fingers through her long black hair. "What kind of tests?"

"Hypnosis susceptibility, brain-wave, ESP and compatibility tests with your counterpart."

"Counterpart?"

"You'll work with a psychically compatible partner, be hypnotized together and asked to carry out joint tasks in an altered state of consciousness."

"Thirty-five dollars a session?"

Nod. "All you have to do is lie back and be hypnotized into ultra-depth. We'll let you know," he said, standing.

In the adjacent room, three students waited to be interviewed.

Jamie recognized Caitlin from journalism class and smiled.

"How many volunteers do they need?" Caitlin asked.

"Four to start. Then, if the results are promising, the original four will be replaced with four new subjects every eight weeks." Jamie took her ski jacket from the coat rack, slipped it on.

"It isn't weird stuff, is it?" Caitlin wrinkled her nose.

"Just testing psychic ability in a deep trance, I think."

"This psychology department has been known to explore some really strange stuff," Caitlin said. Jamie shrugged, waved goodbye.

Jamie's boots echoed in the empty skyway connecting the psychology building with the cafeteria and student lounge. Beyond the floor-to-ceiling glass, the sun appeared, a fiery ball caught in skeletal trees. The snow-covered landscape glowed luminous pink.

In the cafeteria, Jamie purchased black coffee to go, then made her way through the lounge where students gathered around a circular fireplace in the center of the room. The aroma of coffee mingled with the scent of burning oak logs, and she stopped to inhale deeply before leaning into a door that opened onto the parking lot.

"Bessie, please start," she whispered, twisting the ignition key in her 1982 Honda. A low groan became a sputtering cough that finally caught, slamming the loose muffler against the bottom of the vehicle. "Bless you, Bessie." Jamie sat, shoulders hunched, hands hugging the coffee cup, her breath fogging the windshield, waiting for the car to warm up.

Two hundred eighty extra dollars a month would help her to stay in school, but if she were accepted in the ultra-depth program, Trevor would yell about the two nights out each week. Not that he didn't leave her alone more often than not, but logic didn't apply to their relationship. They had met at community college night classes; she was studying data processing, he was learning to use a computer to speed up his construction company's bidding process. They were married in 1989, shortly before the country slid into recession and construction jobs dried up.

After three years of subsistence living and a lot of meditation, Jamie decided to go back to school to study writing and computer programming. Combining the two abilities would somehow result in a high-paying job.

"Where'd you get such a stupid idea?" Trevor said.

"In meditation."

"Weirdo New Age crap. Go by that, you'll end up in a white robe selling flowers on street corners."

She didn't argue with him anymore. Rocks were hard, water was wet, and Trevor was Trevor. In the early days, they talked about having a family and planned to build a house on the banks of Crescent Lake. Today, they seldom had sex and the mention of children was taboo. Jamie decided to create a life of her own.

\* \* \* \* \*

"Your brain wave is alpha seven, just a point off the average," Dr. MacIntyre said, switching on the overhead lights.

Jamie rubbed her eyes. She had been sitting in the dark, staring at a strobing Brain Wave Synchronizer until the color purple appeared within the white illumination.

Doctor Mac, as the students called him, was fifty but looked younger. He had electric blue eyes and curly, gray-streaked brown hair. His attire varied little from day to day: faded Levi's, running shoes, denim shirts, splashy ties and a tweedy sport coat with classic leather elbow patches.

"Is that good or bad?" Jamie said.

Doctor Mac laughed and held up a set of ESP cards. He explained how the test would be conducted and asked Jamie to pull her chair closer to his desk. Then she closed her eyes and began to breathe deeply until he said, "Let's begin."

She waited for words to come into her mind. "Star. Waves. Star. Square."

"Next line."

"Circle. Triangle. Waves. Star."

The test took 20 minutes. When it was over she said, "How did I do?"

"Very well. Tell me about your metaphysical background." He leaned back, lacing his fingers behind his head.

"My dad always said I was a 'great guesser,' but looking back, I think I was being psychic. I don't normally use it on demand, but I do pay attention to my hunches. Plus, I read a lot of metaphysical books; and I'm a novice astrologer."

"What are your feelings about reincarnation?"

"I consider karma my philosophical basis of reality."

Doc Mac smiled. "I want you in the program, Jamie. I'll computer-match you to the other volunteers to come up with your counterpart. Can you begin next Tuesday?"

\* \* \* \* \*

"Well, if you're going to play psychic two nights a week, I guess I'll just spend those nights at the Rodeo Club." Tall and stocky, Trevor leaned against the bedroom door frame looking down at Jamie who sat doing homework at a desk by the window.

She turned to face him. "You already spend a couple of nights a week anyway. We need the money, Trevor."

"We wouldn't if you still worked full time."

"At a dead-end job."

"Welcome to the club," he grumbled, walking away.

\* \* \* \* \*

"Jamie Hamlyn, meet Evan Shipley, your ultra-depth counter-part," Doctor Mac said when she arrived at the psychology department's laboratory.

Evan stood, extending his hand. Tall, thin, his rugged looks were softened by shoulder-length, sand-colored hair. Forty to forty-five, she guessed. Warm smile. "The good doctor has been telling me about you, Jamie."

She smiled. "Then it's my turn to learn about you."

"I'm a lawyer who would rather write books, so I've been taking classes on how to become the next John Grisham."

Doctor Mac added, "And Evan's an alpha six, with an ESP test score identical to yours."

Jamie looked from Doctor Mac to Evan. "I feel like maybe we've met before." She shook her head as if to clear cobwebs.

"Me too, but I didn't want to sound corny," Evan said.

"Did I sound corny?" Jamie asked, smiling.

"No, no, not at all. Not . . ."

"Okay. Take a seat both of you, I'm going to explain the process." Doctor Mac sat on the edge of his desk facing their two chairs. "You'll both sit side by side in lounge chairs, and I'm going to ask you to join hands with a special quartz crystal between your cupped hands."

"What's special about the crystal?" Evan asked.

"It's been programmed to enhance subjective impressions. I'll direct the hypnosis over the sound system and you'll each wear headphones. Following a body relaxation, we'll do a chakra-link. I'll ask you both to imagine an arch of deep purple light connecting the crown chakra of spirituality on the tops of your heads to each other. A blue light will connect your third-eye brow chakras, and a silvery blue light will connect your throat chakras. The link increases the potential of joint explorations. That won't happen tonight unless by some chance you've shared a past life, and even if you have, I won't be directing you to choose a shared incarnation."

Doctor Mac took two glasses of water from the desk, handed one to Jamie, the other to Evan. Next he gave them each a vial of honey and two vitamin E capsules. "The honey and E will help you remain awake and alert for the long induction process. Ultra-depth is a nickname for plenary hypnosis. It takes anywhere from forty-five minutes to two hours to complete the induction. I'll make it interesting by having you imagine different environments enhanced with three-dimensional sound effects."

"You're going to regress us into a past life?" Jamie said.

Nod. "Have either of you been regressed?"

Both Jamie and Evan shook their heads.

"All right, let's get ready. If you need to, go to the bathroom before we begin. The session will be in the next room."

A few minutes later, Jamie and Evan settled into the lounge chairs. While putting on the headphones, their eyes met and they smiled. Evan whispered, "This may be an E-ticket ride."

The tiny room was walnut paneled, overly warm, and dimly lighted. A windowed booth faced the chairs. "Comfy?" the doctor asked as he clipped lapel microphones on the volunteers. They nodded. "I'll direct the process from the booth." He took a double-terminated quartz crystal from his sportcoat pocket and placed it in Evan's hand. Jamie cupped her hand over his. The crystal seemed overly warm; for a fleeting moment she felt dizzy and mentally fought for equilibrium.

She looked at Evan, who appeared equally confused.

"Close your eyes; and let's begin," Doctor Mac said. He stepped into the booth and closed the door.

Jamie closed her eyes, then opened them to see Doctor Mac slide into a chair and begin snapping switches and turning knobs.

"Is this volume acceptable?" he asked. "You can respond verbally."

"Fine."

"Yes."

"All right, it's time to begin to breathe deeply and relax completely. Take a very deep breath, hold it as long as it's comfortable, then let it out slowly through slightly parted teeth. When you feel the breath is all the way out, contract your stomach muscles and push it even further out . . . and then repeat the process."

Jamie felt herself relaxing a little more with each breath. Evan's hand felt warm in hers, and although the crystal felt like a heating element, their hands were not sweating. By the time Doctor Mac had finished the body relaxation and chakra link, Jamie could hardly feel her physical body.

"And it's time to vividly imagine yourself outside on a warm summery day, standing at the top of a stairway that goes down, down, down, twisting around as it goes down, down, down, through the grass and trees, down, down, down . . . and you now vividly imagine yourself going down, down, down the stairs as I count backwards from twenty to one. Vividly imagine going down these stairs that lead eventually to a beautiful garden. Number twenty, down, down, down . . . ."

The garden appeared before her inner eyes as a vivid dream. *As real as if I were here,* she thought, watching butterflies flutter from flower to flower.

The stairway continued down, down, down, until she was in a mountain meadow. She no longer clearly heard Doctor Mac's words, but felt them inside her head, compelling her to act and to see the magically created environment. "In one direction, far below is the ocean, and in the other direction, snow-capped mountains disappear into the distance in diminishing shades of blue."

Jamie felt a breeze in her hair and noted a scent of wild sage. Then to her surprise, she saw someone on the other side of the meadow. It was Evan. She waved. He waved back.

"... and now walk across the meadow to the place where the stairs continue down, down, down."

Evan was ahead of her, waiting at the top of the stairs. When she reached him, he opened his arms, and they hugged like old friends. She looked deeply into his eyes and smiled. He smiled, took her hand and led the way down the stairs. Twenty to one, then a landing. Twenty to one again, over and over, down the stairs holding Evan's hand until they finally reached the beach.

"Go ahead and walk along the beach as a mist rolls in off the sea. It feels good to be here." Overhead Jamie noticed seagulls wheel and dive. Waves rolled across the sand, splashing their feet as they walked hand in hand.

"... and there's a solace in the sound of the surf, a mental tide of tranquillity, as the waves come in and out, leaving in its wake a sense of rediscovered peace ... as you drift deeper and deeper into the deepest possible hypnotic sleep ... sleep .... "

Sandpipers darted in and out of the surf, and in the distance a chain of pelicans skimmed low over the relaxing, rhythmic waves.

"... and you notice among the rocks what appears to be the mouth of a cave, so you decide to go investigate."

She tightened her grip on Evan's hand as they walked to the cave opening.

"... and you know it's perfectly safe to enter the cave ... perfectly safe to enter the darkness where a wonderful adventure awaits. And you're ready to explore, so you boldly enter the cave ... moving from the light into darkness ... deeper and deeper into darkness."

Jamie hesitated. Evan put his arm around her, gently guiding her into the darkness — footsteps echoing — a far-away voice saying, "In the memory banks of your subconscious mind is a recollection of everything that has ever happened to you .... "

Complete blackness.

"... and it's time to bring forgotten awareness to the surface so that you may better understand what influences, restricts or motivates you in the present."

Evan's arm around her felt warm and protective.

". . . as you move through the cave, you begin to see a light in the distance, and as you walk toward the light, your higher mind is choosing a past lifetime that will be of value for you to explore at this time."

They approached the light together.

"Number two . . . and as you step out of the cave on the count of one, you'll perceive yourself in an important situation in this past lifetime. Number one."

Jamie turned to Evan . . . Eva—no no . . . Joshua. Joshua yelling at her. "Damn it, Pauline, what do you expect?"

"I expect you to treat her nicer," Pauline said, turning to look down the stairs and across the boardwalk to where her best friend stood crying beneath the flashing ballroom sign. Beyond was the pier, black waves reflecting fragments of moonlight. Palm fronds rustled in the warm breeze, barely heard over trombones and saxophones.

"You know how she treats me." Sadness in Joshua's voice.

"I'll talk to her," Pauline said. Lifting the hem of her dress, she descended the stairs. Joshua and Sarah brought out the worst in each other. They fought, broke up, and got back together as regularly as most people took out the garbage.

"Are you all right?" Pauline put her arm around Sarah.

"I hate him."

"You have to accept him the way he is, Sarah."

"If he loved me, he'd change."

"What if he asked that of you?"

"Are you taking his side?" Sarah said, pulling away and glaring at Pauline.

"I'm trying to be your friend."

"The two of you would get along great."

"Sarah, that's uncalled for. Let's go to the ladies' room and redo your makeup."

Sarah looked up the stair landing to see Joshua watching them. Face clouded in anger, she grabbed Pauline's arm, and growled, "Come on."

"Sarah, that hurts. What's wrong with you?"

"Come on."

Without resisting, Pauline allowed herself to be led up to where Joshua waited.

Trembling, Sarah grasped Joshua's hand and slammed Pauline's hand into his. "Here! I give you each other—a union sealed by fate." Turning, laughing maniacally, Sarah bolted down the stairs, tripping once and catching herself. Once on the boardwalk, she kicked off her shoes and began to run toward the pier.

"Joshua?"

"Let her go. When she gets like this there's no reasoning with her, you know that."

They watched her run down the nearly deserted pier, past the merry-go-round and game booths to the railing, which she proceeded to climb. Teetering on the top rail, she turned, looked up at Joshua and Pauline. Slowly extending her arms, Christ-like, she fell backward into the dark water.

When Pauline screamed, Jamie trembled in the lounge chair. Doctor Mac didn't notice. He sat in the control booth preparing to voice the next suggestions.

Sirens. They were standing in the sand surrounded by a semi-circle of people in party attire, speaking in hushed whispers. Joshua was wet, shivering as he held Pauline in his arms. Flashlights. Shouting. Men carrying Sarah out of the surf. A white sheet was placed over her body.

Pauline felt dizzy and began spiraling into darkness to the up-tempo beat of the Charleston. The music faded away and the midnight sky turned to indigo, to blue. She was leaving the funeral . . . driving . . . talking with friends, Sarah's parents, she was so sorry—the same words over and over again. Escaping to the yard, she noticed Joshua in the gazebo.

Wearing a long black dress, Pauline sat on the loveseat, drew her knees to her chest, and locked her arms around her legs. The breeze blew her chestnut locks across her face. Below, stretching for miles, Los Angeles glistened in the afternoon sun.

"Do you want to know what set her off, Pauline?"

"Does it matter, Joshua?"

"After we were supposed to get married next spring, she wanted me to work for her father. I told her I wanted to work for myself." Joshua, dressed in a black suit, walked to the edge of the yard and stared into the distance.

"Sarah was high strung. Everything took on more importance than it deserved," Pauline said, massaging her temples.

"But I feel so guilty," he said, turning to face her.

"Me too, and neither of us have reason."

Strolling back to the gazebo, he sat across from her, and placed his hand on her hand. "Before she jumped, did she bless us or curse us?"

"She was just being dramatic like the women in moving pictures."

"Someday I'll tell you . . ."

From far away, another voice intruded, saying, "It's time to let go of this and return to the present. On the count of three you'll be back in the present, remembering everything that you just experienced. You'll remain in a deep, altered state of consciousness, but back in the present. Number one."

Jamie felt herself float off the loveseat and begin to spiral through time and space into a limbo world where she was being instructed to awaken, at peace with herself, the world and everyone in it.

". . . and number five, wide awake. Open your eyes and feel good."

Jamie opened her eyes to see Doctor Mac step out of the control booth. She turned to look at Evan, met his eyes and shivered.

"How are you doing?" Doctor Mac said, unclasping the lapel microphones.

Jamie nodded, trying to find her voice.

"Did you both have vivid experiences?"

"It was as real as this," Evan said, pinching his own arm.

"Me too," Jamie said.

"Don't compare notes about what you experienced. Not here or anywhere else. Agreed? And I'd like you to use the last forty-five minutes of the session to write a detailed report." He handed them both a clipboard. "Take a few moments to stretch, then use the desks in the next room."

Jamie looked at her watch. "We were in hypnosis two hours

and fifteen minutes?"

"Seemed like a few minutes," Evan said.

Reports completed, they left the building together. "I'd love to buy you a cup of coffee," Evan said. "The Campus Cafe on Main Street?"

Jamie hesitated. She wanted to accept. Trevor wouldn't be home before midnight. Her homework was finished. "That would be nice. Will you wait to make sure my car starts."

The aroma of grilled onions and the sound of soft-rock music wafted out the front door of the cafe. Students in brightly-colored ski jackets were arriving, leaving. Some hunched over coffee. Others cuddled together, studying. Jamie and Evan made their way to a back booth.

"We're the oldest ones here," Evan said.

"I'm used to it," Jamie replied.

They ordered coffee and decided to share a piece of pecan pie.

"I've never experienced anything like it," he said.

Jamie smiled, shook her head. "Wish we could talk about it."

"One of the people in the regression was my ex-wife."

"We can't compare notes."

"I'm just offering an unsettling statement of fact."

"But she looked different?" Jamie couldn't help but ask.

He lifted the mug to his lips and looked at Jamie over the top of the steaming cup. "Soul recognition, maybe. I knew it was her."

"Karma, huh?"

"I'm letting go. Our only problem today is over visitations with my six-year-old son."

"What's his name?"

"Joshua. Too Biblical for me, but Susan insisted." Evan slipped a billfold from his hip pocket and opened it to show a photo of a smiling blond-haired boy standing next to his kneeling mother.

Jamie shuddered.

"I understand you're divorced, too, Jamie. How long?"

"Uh, not long. Do you really want to write novels?"

"A good lawyer is aggressive, which takes too much out of me. Writing is pure pleasure."

"I'm studying journalism and non-fiction writing in hopes of combining wise words with computer programming."

"Why not?" Evan toasted with his mug. "To our writing careers."

\* \* \* \* \*

"We may have accidentally happened upon a unique situation," Doctor Mac said to Jamie and Evan at the beginning of the Thursday night session. He was holding the separate reports each had written following the first experience.

"Do you believe in accidents, Doctor?" Evan said.

Doctor Mac met Evan's eyes and slowly shook his head. "My research assures me that destiny is always in play when it comes to important encounters."

"Can you tell us about it?" Jamie said.

"Soon. But let's do a session now."

Minutes later, Doctor Mac was counting them down the long twisting stairs to the garden. Joshua was there. They hugged, laughed and enjoyed the idyllic environment. After descending to the mountain meadow, instead of lingering as instructed, they went directly down the many flights of stairs to the beach, where they built a sand castle until instructed to go to the cave.

"Push, my dear, push!"

Pauline opened her eyes to see a ceiling fan spinning above. Joshua held her hand, saying, "You're doing fine." She was lying on her back, legs in the air, covered with a sheet. A nurse patted her on the arm and smiled.

I'm having a baby. My God, I'm having a baby. The realization overwhelmed her.

"Push, Pauline," a man said.

Moments after the baby's first cry, Joshua kneeled beside her. "We have a son, Pauline." Tears welled in his eyes.

As the nurse laid the baby in her arms, the environment began to swirl around her, moving from light to darkness to light again, and finally stabilizing into a Spanish-style living room. It was night. Fireplace embers glowed orange. The baby cooed at her breast. "Auld Lang Syne" played on the radio, and Joshua leaned down to kiss her on the lips, saying, "Happy New Year, my love."

"Happy 1925, Joshua," she whispered. "And Happy New Year to you, my little James Charles Monet." She kissed the baby on the head.

"It's going to be a wonderful year . . . year . . . year . . . year . . ."

"Where's Joshua? I can't believe he's late for James Charles' sixth birthday party," said a white-haired woman carrying a tray of cookies to the garden table.

Pauline stood in the midst of a dozen children, directing a game — twirling a blindfolded little girl three times before pointing her in the direction of a donkey sketched upon the trunk of a palm tree.

She looked up minutes later to see the white-haired woman talking to a policeman. He nodded, turned his head and walked in her direction.

"Husband . . . accident . . . sorry." The key words hit her like bomb fragments, knocking her to the ground and dragging her soul into darkness.

". . . number five, wide awake. Wide awake. Open your eyes and feel good."

Jamie opened her eyes, looked at Evan, and burst into tears. Putting his arms around her, he whispered, "I know, I know."

Doctor Mac's concerned pleas were unheard.

"You died on me . . . Joshua died on me and we had such a wonderful —"

"Please, I need separate reports," Doctor Mac interrupted.

Jamie pulled away from Evan and turned to Doctor Mac. "No separate reports. We need to talk about this."

"But for the sake of the research . . ."

"Our Tuesday reports were identical, weren't they, Doctor?" Evan said.

"Yes, but —"

"And they'll be identical tonight," Evan said. "So wouldn't research be better served by verbally comparing experiences while they're still fresh in our minds?"

Doctor Mac tape-recorded Jamie and Evan's story, which took nearly an hour to relate. "It's not unusual for couples to interact in plenary hypnosis, but not this fast. They also occasionally tune out the hypnotist and go off on their own as you did in skipping the mountain meadow experience to build a sand castle on the beach. After another session or two, you may not need me at all." Leaning back in his chair, Doctor Mac looked from Jamie to Evan. "I think the two of you shared a 1920s incarnation . . . that somehow destiny arranged this present meeting."

"At this moment," Jamie swallowed hard, "I feel like we're still back there in the twenties. I as Pauline, feel I'm deeply in love with Joshua . . . and we should now go home together." She looked at Evan. "Sorry, but I think it needs to be said."

"I feel exactly the same way." Evan took her hand.

"This is why I insist volunteers be unattached," Doctor Mac said. "The plenary bonding factor has been intensified by your spiritual lineage."

"What's a plenary bonding factor?" Jamie said.

"Over a period of time, subjects who share this experience tend to bond. The initial Northern California university experiments were responsible for a lot of divorces."

Jamie repressed any visible reaction, but felt her stomach tighten.

"What will we explore in the next session, Doctor?" Evan said.

Doctor Mac shook his head. "This situation is so unique I'll create something special."

Jamie and Evan left together. Without speaking, they crossed the skyway and descended the stairs to the nearly deserted student lounge. Oak logs smoldered in the circular fireplace. Evan took Jamie's hand, led her to a bench by the hearth.

Staring at the glowing embers, he said, "My ex-wife in this life was Sarah in the twenties incarnation. You and I were later married. I was killed in an auto accident, leaving you with a son the same age as my son now. Why? What the hell is going on?"

She shrugged, didn't reply.

"I've known you three days. And I love you, Jamie. Maybe our experiences accelerated the process, but I would have loved you anyway." He placed his hands gently on her cheeks, leaned forward, and kissed her on the lips.

Shocked by her own eager response, Jamie gave herself freely to the passion of the kiss.

"Jamie, I—"

"Evan, I'm married." The words released a floodgate, and tears filled her eyes. "I have to go."

\* \* \* \* \*

When Jamie didn't show up for the Tuesday evening ultra-depth session, Doctor Mac called her home. "This is Steven MacIntyre at the college. Is Jamie there?"

"Doctor Mac, right?" Trevor said.

"That's what the students call me."

"My wife's always been a New Age loon, but you pushed her over the edge, pal."

"Your wife?"

"She's in California checking out her past lives, if you can believe that."

"Do you have a number where I can call her?"

"Hell, no!"

"Do you know when she'll be back?"

"Whenever she does, she'd better have an explanation for all this crap!"

"When she returns, please have her call me." Doctor Mac hung up the phone and turned to Evan.

\* \* \* \* \*

Friday afternoon, Jamie sat at a table on the Santa Monica pier reading grainy photocopies from microfiche records of newspaper stories she had already read a dozen times.

### July 27, 1922
## Suicide at the
## Byzantine La Monica Ballroom

Last night at 11:30, after a fight with her boy-friend, 21-year-old Sarah Dever of Venice jumped from the Santa Monica Pier into the bay. Her body was found two hours later by . . .

*New Arrivals—December 16, 1924*
# James Charles Monet
# Born to Joshua and Pauline Monet

Joshua Monet is a cub reporter for this news-paper. The happy parents reside in Santa Monica. Their seven-pound, three-ounce son arrived . . .

---

*December 16, 1930*
# Joshua Dean Monet
# Killed in Auto Accident

Popular columnist Joshua Monet was killed when a car ran a red light at Pacific Coast Highway and the California Incline, striking Monet's vehicle . . .

---

Jamie sipped coffee from a paper cup, closed her eyes and relished the sunshine and warm breeze off the sea. She noted the scents of popcorn, hot dogs and fish-and-chips. The merry-go-round's calliope filled the air with music from another, all too familiar era.

Picking up the next newspaper story, she read:

*March 24, 1931*
# Pauline Monet to
# Continue Her Husband's Column,
# Beginning Today

Following the tragic accidental death in December of popular columnist Joshua Monet, his wife Pauline decided to continue her husband's work. As our readers will remember, Monet featured human-interest stories emphasizing positive aspects of Los Angeles.

Pauline Monet's first column (Page 13) documents the efforts of Sister Mary Therese of the St. Vincent's Orphanage. In this initial offering . . .

---

"Can I sit down?"

Jamie turned in her chair to see Evan standing, silhouetted against the sun.

"Evan, how did you—" She jumped to her feet and threw her arms around him. He lifted her off the ground and spun her around.

"Private detectives. Use them all the time in my work."

"But how, in such a big city?"

"Believe it or not, there aren't many people researching the 1920s at the *Los Angeles Times* or in the UCLA research library."

"You traced my identification to check out the microfiche? But that was three days ago!" Jamie said, amazed.

Holding her tightly around the waist, Evan pointed to a man in a sport coat standing by the merry-go-round.

"I've been followed?" she laughed.

"Didn't want to lose you."

"I feel at home here, Evan."

"So do I."

"I'm not going back."

"Okay."

"Okay, what?"

"Then I'm not going back either."

"Can you do that?"

"Don't they need lawyers in Los Angeles?"

"No, Evan. They need writers . . . like you."

"We might starve."

"We won't."

"You sure?"

"I have an idea for a newspaper column . . . ."

# If Reality Is Illusion, Where Does That Leave Me?

## 1

It started the day Julie ran over Rufus. She cried. The children cried. The family tragedy inspired lengthy discussions about values, priorities, the purpose of life, the meaning of death.

I thought the traumatic impact on our lives would subside within a day or two.

It didn't.

Instead, the cat's demise became the impetus for our spiritual quest—our summons to cross the Atlantic on the Titanic. Had Rufus lived, I'd still be working as an art director in a Los Angeles ad agency instead of sitting on a meditation pillow in a mountain-top monastery, contemplating things we were never meant to question.

But I'm getting ahead of myself.

Looking back, destiny began rerouting our path on the afternoon of Rufus' funeral. Sue Lynne, eight, and James Byron, six, carried the casket, a plastic laundry detergent bucket. I dug a hole behind the rose bushes. Julie carried the marker—a wooden plaque nailed to a stick. Sue Lynne used her wood-burning set to register Rufus' approximate date of birth and exact date of death.

Julie read an appropriate passage from a book of New Age prayers. Everyone cried, including me. As I shoveled dirt over the plastic casket, Sue Lynne held my waist, James Byron clutched one of my legs; both were sobbing and wiping their noses on my clothes.

When the burial was complete, I said, "Maybe we can go to the Pizza Palace for lunch, reminisce about Rufus."

"While stuffing our stomachs?" Sue Lynne sobbed, rushing into the house.

"I'm going to wait for Rufus to come back," James Byron said, sitting in the grass facing the grave.

My heart sank. "Rufus isn't coming back, Son." I sat beside him, put my arm around his shoulders.

"He'll reincarnate, then we'll dig him up."

I looked up at my wife standing beside us.

"Reincarnate?"

"Mom said Rufus will reincarnate as a kitten."

"Reincarnation is a nice idea," Julie said, looking at me apologetically over our son's head.

"Son, I don't know about reincarnation, but I know if Rufus comes back, it won't be in the bucket we just buried."

"Where then?" James Byron scanned the yard for an appropriate place.

I patted my son, stood, and faced my wife. "Julie, we need to talk." We strolled to the patio, sat in deck chairs facing the rock garden.

"Reincarnation?" I said.

"Last night, when I was so upset, I called Martha. She's a Theosophist. She explained how reincarnation works and told me stories about animals returning to their owners. This morning, she brought me this book of prayers." She held the volume to her chest.

"Crissake, Julie, reincarnation is for Hindus."

"We've ignored our spirituality, Dylan." Julie's eyes were misting. "And our children's spirituality."

"I don't think we're any the worse because of it."

"Until something like this happens!" The mist became a deluge. Julie rushed into the house.

James Byron sat in the yard waiting for Rufus to return.

I twisted the top off a longneck Coors, surveyed my landscaped suburban backyard, and sighed.

## 2

The Lakers were behind one point in the closing moments of the game when Julie handed me a paperback book: *Reincarnation: Questions and Answers.*

I held the book as if it didn't exist, my attention still riveted to the TV screen.

"You have to read it, Dylan."

I think I nodded. Shaquille O'Neal sprinted across the court and was just spinning the ball into the air when Julie punched the remote control, killing the picture.

"Sports aren't spiritual, Dylan."

"Julie, what the hell is wrong with you? The Lakers are as spiritual as it gets." Grabbing the remote, I resurrected the TV. Game scores from other cities rolled over a wide shot of the court. The game was over.

"Reality isn't what you perceive it to be, Dylan."

"I sure wish you hadn't run over Rufus, Julie." I flipped the book into her lap. "You've been weird for weeks."

"Rufus died to save us, Dylan."

I looked at my wife in disbelief. "What? Christ Cat?"

"Because of his death, I'm asking questions that need to be answered."

"Like what?"

"Like why I am here?"

I waited for more, but that was it. "You're here to fix lunch."

"I'm serious, Dylan."

"So am I." The final score of the Lakers game never appeared on the screen.

"I want to know why I'm here on earth. What's my karma? What's my dharma?"

"Maybe Martha knows. Ask her." A golf tournament started. Yawn. I turned off the TV.

"Dylan, fix your own lunch."

"Julie, you're a cosmic dingbat," I yelled as she left the room.

Instead of the usual ham or turkey, the refrigerator was filled with tofu, goat milk, alfalfa sprouts, and eight varieties of fruit. In the bread box, my fluffy white bread had turned into wholegrain, peppered with birdseed. I fixed a can of soup and ate an apple.

While clearing the dining room table, Julie joined me in the kitchen. "We have to talk," she said.

"Agreed." I opened the refrigerator and pointed.

"The vibrational frequency of our diet was unacceptable."

I didn't know what to say.

"Meat is at the bottom of the spiritual chain."

I found my voice. "SCREW THE SPIRITUAL CHAIN. WHAT ABOUT FOOD VALUE?"

"You'll be healthier as a vegetarian."

"I'M NOT A VEGETARIAN."

"From this moment on, I'll be cooking only vegetarian meals. You, of course, are free to eat elsewhere or cook for yourself."

The transition took three months. My meat meal was lunch with fellow art directors at restaurants near the agency. Dinner was "tofu surprise" or peeled grapes wrapped in lettuce leaves. I lost ten pounds. Julie lost five. Sue Lynne and James Byron complained but adapted.

At this point in my story, I should probably provide some family background.

Julie and I met at Los Angeles Art Center School fifteen years ago. During the first week of school, while I was presenting my design concepts, Julie raised her hand to offer criticism. I hated her on sight. But she was right; the instructor agreed. We were married two years later. Following graduation, I took an art director position at a West L.A. ad agency. Julie joined a Venice studio, specializing in fashion illustration.

When Sue Lynne was born, Julie freelanced from home. After James Byron arrived, she gave up illustration to become a full-time mother, PTA volunteer, room mother, Girl Scout leader, and carpool coordinator, balancing Sue Lynne's ballet and tennis lessons with James Byron's nursery school and her own aerobic exercise classes and running schedule.

Allow for a little prejudice on my part when I say that Julie is a woman who turns mens' heads hard enough to give them whiplash. Miss Pasadena at age nineteen, today at thirty-five she looks twenty-five. Slim, with blue eyes, blond hair cut and styled to achieve a care-free look, Julie projects sophistication and seductiveness.

We always figured we were soulmates. After thirteen years of marriage, life was relaxed, predictable, and pleasurable. We seldom fought. Family birthdays and holidays were highlights. We looked forward to vacations, get-togethers with friends, new plays, movies, art shows, and concerts. I never cheated on Julie. I don't think she ever cheated on me. Funny that I mention that. Before Kafka, I wouldn't have. But I'm getting ahead of myself again.

Because I love my wife, I tried to be supportive of her metaphysical obsession. Since the day Rufus "crossed over," as Julie refers to it, I've read twelve New Age books. I've learned more than I ever wanted to know about divination, psychic ability, reincarnation, shamanism, angels, and channeling. I'm supposed to be creating my own reality, but to tell the truth, my reality was perfectly acceptable during the days when Rufus walked the earth.

Together, Julie and I attended an after-death seminar, a human-potential seminar, and three channeling sessions. That's where I met Kafka: a Jesus Christ look-like—long hair, white robe, the whole show.

Julie introduced us. "Dylan, Kafka."

Kafka brought his hands together as if to pray and bowed his head. I nodded. He took Julie's hand, kissed it passionately. "Your wife is an ethereal soul," he said, staring into her eyes like a lost puppy. "You were magnificent last night," he whispered.

Kafka turned to me. "You don't mind us having astral sex?"

Julie blushed. "In our dreams, Dylan. Out of body, you know."

"As long as there's no fluid exchange," I said, puzzled and a tad annoyed, if truth be told.

"Kafka channels a spirit named Zantoff—an ancient Spartan warrior," Julie said.

Kafka waited. I shrugged. "Good qualification for guiding modern man on his spiritual search."

"Yes," Kafka said, "oh, yes."

The session took place in the guru's Venice apartment; art deco meets east India. Candlelight. Incense. We sat on uncomfortable card-table chairs—twenty seekers of light, encircling Kafka on a pillow in yoga position. Five minutes of silence. Then channeled words from an entity in spirit. Soft at first. Louder. Halting. Bela Lugosi with a lisp.

In a nutshell, his message could be summarized as "wisdom erases karma," but it took him ninety minutes to get it out. My mind wandered. My butt ached. At this very moment, a new Sydney Pollack film was playing in Westwood. A Fritz Scholder show was opening at the museum. Hell, MTV was better than this.

"I leave you now in the spirit of love." Kafka shivered, spasmed, opened his eyes.

"Well, how was it?" he said, dazed.

The observers applauded, murmured. Women rushed to hug the channeler. When it was Julie's turn, Kafka held her longer, whispered in her ear, allowed his hand to roam dangerously close to her buttocks.

Another husband, sensing a kindred spirit, whispered, "You buy into that bull?"

"My wife thinks it's wonderful."

"Mine too. I think"—he glanced in her direction—"she's lost an oar." He introduced himself. Harvey.

I smiled.

Harvey said, "They say he does them all."

"What?"

"The women who come to him for private sessions are bestowed with divine direction and holy sperm."

"No?"

"That's what I hear."

I pondered the possibilities and settled on denial.

The evening ended with a Kafka prayer. Donations were collected at the door on the way out. I resisted depositing $20 in the tip jar. Julie insisted.

During the short drive home, I asked my wife if she'd ever had a private session with Kafka.

"Three times. He's the best."

I swallowed hard.

"Only Brother John is said to be better."

"Brother John?"

"He's offering a two-week retreat next month at Mt. Shasta."

## 3

"We could be going to Club Med," I mumbled, standing in line holding the boarding passes for a flight to San Francisco.

Julie squeezed my hand. "You promised, Dylan. I could have gone alone, but you said, 'No, no, I want to go too.' You promised not to complain, remember?"

A voice crackled over the US Airways sound system. "We are now boarding rows five through twelve."

Julie and I moved past the gate attendant down the ramp to the plane. I wondered again about my real motivation for accompanying my wife. Could she resist a charming psychic seducer? Of course she could.

Once settled onboard the plane, Julie took a brochure from her purse and handed it to me. TWO WEEKS OF MEDITATION AND SELF-EXPLORATION. The type arched over the head of a smiling, bearded, bald-headed man in a grey robe.

"Brother John looks stoned," I said.

"Bliss, Dylan, bliss. He meditates."

"More channeling?" I asked.

Julie shook her head. "Brother John was a psychiatrist who refused to accept the unrealistic restrictions of his profession."

"What does that mean?"

"He left psychiatry to start a religion."

I looked at my wife.

Nodding, smiling serenely, she said, "The Brotherhood of Mystic Insight."

I opened the brochure. STUDENTS WILL ARISE AT 4 AM. GRUEL WILL BE SERVED AT 4:30 AM. SILENT BREAKFAST IN THE MAIN DINING ROOM.

The plane taxied down the runway and lifted into the smog-shrouded sky. Exactly on time the one time I was in no hurry to get where I was going.

"A silent breakfast of gruel, served at 4:30 AM?"

Julie nodded while watching the Malibu coastline disappear beneath us.

"What's gruel, and why can't we talk?"

"You know gruel is porridge, Dylan. And you can't talk because you're supposed to live in the *now*. If you're going to eat, eat. Don't eat and talk. Focus on eating."

"That's nuts."

"*Now* is all you ever have."

"Sunday nights, we used to eat in the TV room, watch a show, talk, referee the children . . . all at the same time."

"Exactly."

I waited. Nothing.

"Julie?"

"Dylan, when you do more than one thing at a time you can't be with the primary task. You never *flow*."

Rather than argue, I read the brochure.

STUDENTS WILL SIT IN SILENT MEDITATION FOR FIVE HOURS A DAY. AT THE END OF EACH SESSION, EVERYONE IS EXPECTED TO VOLUNTEER THREE HOURS OF SERVICE IN THE KITCHEN OR VEGETABLE GARDEN.

The idea of using my precious two-week vacation to stare at the wall and work in a vegetable garden was ludicrous. I wanted to cry. But after hearing Harvey's speculations, it was better than having Julie go alone.

Julie read over my shoulder. "Brother John will also process us for two hours a day," she said. There was a long silence. "Do you know what 'process' means, Dylan?"

I shook my head.

"Ask questions, sometimes in an altered state. He'll ask questions about our lives and ask us to go within to find answers."

"Five hours of meditation, three hours of manual labor, two hours of processing. Ten hours? We won't have any time to ourselves."

"And we go to bed early." She pointed to the words.

"Bunk beds in a cubicle?"

She nodded.

"All for only $2,000 each?"

"Isn't it wonderful?"

In San Francisco we caught a commuter flight to Redding where we rented a car for the 90-minute drive to Brother John's center.

"Is it a commune?" I asked.

"Sincere followers are accepted to live full time at the center."

Leaving Interstate 5, the road became a narrow ribbon of blacktop. "Feel the mellow vibrations," Julie said as we snaked our way up the mountain through sugar pines, quaking aspen and white fir. "It's a sacred site." she added.

"It's a mountain."

"It's sacred. Everyone knows it."

"Who knows?"

"Dylan! Mount Shasta is like Sedona, or Stonehenge. The mountain is 14,162 feet high with the cleanest air in the country at the peak."

"Because it's sacred?"

Julie ignored my sarcasm. She was reading the map on the back of the brochure. "Take the next right."

The side road led to the entrance of The Brotherhood of Mystic Insight Center — a long driveway lined with pine trees, limbs entwined overhead like a tunnel. We pulled into a partially-filled parking area. Atop an incline sat a house that looked like it belonged on an Addams Family movie set. Beyond the house, thousands of feet above, the snow-covered mountain peak glowed pink in the afternoon sun.

Stepping out of the car, I inhaled the aroma of pine trees and a hint of woodsmoke. Julie turned full circle, looking up in awe. "We're going to be reborn, Dylan."

"Welcome, Julie and Dylan," said a man in a grey robe who appeared out of nowhere. Long dark hair, about thirty-five, handsome, holding his hands in prayer position. "I am Brother Thomas."

"How did you know our names?" I asked.

"You're the last to arrive," he said, taking Julie's hand in his, bowing and kissing her fingers, one at a time.

"You're not going to do that to me, are you?" I said, extending my hand.

Brother Thomas smiled and shook my hand. "No, only the ladies receive special treatment at The Brotherhood of Mystic Insight."

What did he mean by that? Before I had time to consider the possibilities, Brother Thomas picked up our suitcases and asked us to follow him. The winding path to the house was edged with flowers.

The front doors opened into a massive foyer that smelled of incense. "One moment," he said, taking a key from his robe pocket and unlocking a closet door at the foot of the stairway. He placed our suitcases inside and locked the door.

"I don't understand," I said.

"We provide everything you'll need." He drew his hands into prayer position, bowed and winked at Julie. I think she winked back.

"But I brought along magazines to read, a book. My electric shaver, antacids, underwear . . ."

"You won't need them."

"My Walkman, tapes, reading glasses . . ." My voice sounded pathetic; a pleading child.

Brother Thomas shook his head in an exaggerated gesture of sadness.

"You'll survive, Dylan," said Julie, patting my shoulder.

We followed Brother Thomas up the stairway. An ornate, hand-carved banister curved up to a landing where an ivory Buddha statue sat on an altar surrounded by white candles. On the wall hung a mosaic pentagram.

"Permanent members of the Brotherhood live on the second floor," said Brother Thomas.

At the third floor, we proceeded down a dimly-lighted hallway to a tiny room. On the wall were two narrow bunk beds. No dresser. No bathroom facilities. A small window.

"Your robes and sandals are on the beds, the bathroom is down the hallway to the right. Please change so I can escort you to your duty posts. You're allowed to wear your wedding rings, but I'll take your watches and all other jewelry."

I decided to hold my tongue and wait for Brother Thomas to leave.

"If you'll change into your robes, I'll take your things and put them away for safekeeping."

"You're going to watch us change clothes?" The words sputtered out of my mouth.

"Please don't be bashful. We'll be bathing together in the communal spa and dancing naked around a bonfire next Wednesday evening." Brother Thomas took a folded manila envelope from his pocket, opened it wide, and thrust it in my direction. "For your wallet and jewelry."

Julie laughed. "Dylan, we're in a spiritual center, with spiritual people." She unclasped her necklace and dropped it into the envelope, then proceeded to unbutton her blouse, take it off and fold it neatly on the bed. A moment later she was out of her bra and stepping out of her skirt.

I watched, mouth open, while my naked wife neatly folded and assembled her attire, placed her purse on top, then proudly presented the stack to a smiling Brother Thomas. She slipped the grey robe over her head, adjusted it, tied the sash and said, "Dylan!"

I faced the other way, undressed and quickly put on the robe.

Clutching our belongings to his belly, Brother Thomas said, "Sister Julie, Brother Dylan, please follow me."

## 4

After what I estimated to be two hours of hoeing weeds in a potato patch, a bell rang in the distance. The man two rows away straightened up, thrust his shoulders back and moaned. Turning to me he extended his hand. "We can talk now."

I stepped over potato plants and shook his hand, wincing when his firm grip crushed my blisters. "Brother Peter," he said.

"Dylan . . . uh, Brother Dylan."

Peter laughed and held up a finger as if to say, "Don't forget the Brother bit."

"We have ten minutes to wash up at the well. Then it's dinner in the main room."

"How do you know?" I asked.

"Second time here. My wife's idea of a vacation."

Men in grey robes were walking toward the well from different parts of the immense garden. Two men emerged from the apple trees holding hands. At the well, a big-bellied man used a hand pump to fill a cattle-watering trough.

"Brother Dylan, this is Brother Benton. He lives at the center."

Brother Benton kept pumping, but switched hands to shake mine. Soon, six workers were gathered around the trough, robes off, washing as best we could in the chilly water. The two gay men, Daniel and Troy, were Los Angeles restaurant owners. Peter was a Seattle architect. Maurice, a New York book editor. Owen, a Redding doughnut-shop owner, was a filler.

"What's a filler?" I asked.

"Brother John likes six men and six women for his retreats. When the registration doesn't work out even, I get to fill in for free. A lesbian couple balanced out Daniel and Troy, but I was invited to balance out a single gal."

"You enjoy these retreats that much?"

"Spirituality turns women on, Brother Dylan." Owen, an average-looking forty-year-old with short red hair, raised his eyebrows and smiled like a sly fox. "Women figure whatever they do in such holy surroundings must be divinely inspired."

Brother Benton interrupted. "Dinner," he said, and gestured for us to follow him back to the house.

In a corner of the main dining room, Julie and five women listened to Brother Thomas explain the inner workings of the Brother-hood. I caught her eye and waved. She smiled, returning her attention to the speaker.

The dining tables formed a U-shape around a podium. I counted twenty-four chairs. Dark wood and a beamed ceiling accented the white walls, which were covered with prints of visionary art. A picture window beyond the podium framed Mt. Shasta.

Brother Thomas raised his hands in the air, said, "Can I have your attention, please. At all meals, one of the Brothers or Sisters of Mystic Insight will sit between each of you. After Brother John's welcoming talk, we will eat in silence."

Brother Thomas took a seat beside Julie. I sat between Brother Benton, the pumper, and Sister DeWill, a slight woman with wire-rimmed glasses and a vacant stare. When everyone was seated, a huge man entered the room and walked to the podium. I recognized his bald head and stoned expression from the brochure.

Stroking his beard, Brother John visually swept the room, meeting our eyes before grasping the podium with both hands and speaking in a voice that resonated with authority. "Welcome, Brothers and Sisters, I am Brother John. I know you are here because you want to grow spiri-tually, and the Brothers and Sisters of Mystic Insight are here to help you rise above your fears and become all you can be. For most of you, the journey begins with exploring who you are and what is keeping you from becoming what you want to be."

Brother John sipped from a water glass and continued. "For the two weeks we'll be sharing, the day begins here in the dining room each morning at four-thirty for breakfast. Sitting meditation at five-thirty. Lunch at eleven. Duty post from noon to three. Dharma talks at three-fifteen. Dinner at six, followed by a contemplation period and an hour in the spa." He took a deep breath, smiled, added, "I know you don't have watches, but the Brothers and Sisters and the announcement bell will guide your activities."

Brother John said a prayer, blessed the food, and took his place at the table. The Brothers and Sisters on kitchen duty began to serve the meal—steamed garden vegetables, black bread and herbal tea. Period. I knew better than to hope for meat, but I expected something more— maybe a dish of non-fat ice cream or at least a cup of coffee.

The ping of forks hitting ceramic was the only sound in the room. Wanting to be a good sport, I tried to focus only upon eating. It didn't work. Eating steamed vegetables is probably as boring as life gets. My mind wandered. Obviously, handsome Brother Thomas, who had already seen Julie naked, liked her a lot. And it seemed to me that Julie liked Brother Thomas, too. In trying to figure out which of the six women attendees was single and heterosexual, I settled upon the petite, green-eyed brunette sitting across the table and down a couple spaces. Someone had called her Maria. She noticed me watching and smiled in response.

The meal ended with another prayer and an announcement from Brother Thomas. "You have a half hour to go to your rooms and contemplate the day. Then we'll meet in the spa. Towels will be provided."

"Can you believe all the harmonious vibrations?" Julie mused as we climbed the stairs to the third floor.

"I have blisters on my hands. My back is killing me."

"Hard work feeds the spirit."

"Steamed, spiceless vegetables isn't my idea of a meal."

"Your cholesterol will drop thirty points."

There was no lock on the door of our cubicle. "You okay with the top bunk?" I said.

Without replying, Julie climbed the ladder and sat with her feet dangling over the edge. I fell upon the bottom bunk, closed my eyes and thought about how weird it felt to walk around in a robe without underwear.

"From the kitchen window, I watched you working in the garden," she said. "I was grinding grain for gruel."

"Did Brother Thomas show you how?"

"As a matter of fact, he did."

"He likes you."

"He likes everyone."

"Are we going skinny dipping?"

"We're going to soak in the spa."

"I've never been into nudism."

"Celebrating the divinity of our bodies in a spiritual oasis is not nudism, Dylan."

"Are the Brothers and Sisters of Mystic Insight celibate?"

Julie laughed. "Their beliefs are culled from earth religions. They're loving pagans."

"What does that mean?"

"They're very open sexually. Even most of those in a bonded relationship practice panfidelity."

"Wha—"

Someone knocked on the cubicle door. "Spa time."

I sat up, winced at the pain in my back. "Is panfidelity what I think it is?"

"Faithful non-monogamy. Consensual open sexuality," Julie said as casually as if relating a grocery list.

I swallowed hard, considering words I decided not to say. "That's pretty far-out, Julie, I . . ."

"I used to think so, too," she said, bouncing off the top bunk and extending her hand. "Come on, if we're late, everyone else will watch us parade naked into the spa."

## 5

Twenty-two people watched Julie and me remove our robes and descend the steps into the steaming, rock-lined pool. My fear of getting an erection proved unfounded. Everyone was talking, gesturing—

making up for all the silence, I assumed. Peter introduced me to his wife Laura. She sat neck-deep in the frothing water, but ascended like a leviathan, throwing her arms around me in a belly-button to belly-button hug to end all hugs.

"We-e-elcome," Laura said.

"Thank you."

"I like your wife. We ground grain together." She was holding me tightly.

I gently pulled back, nodded, smiled, said, "This is certainly a different kind of vacation."

"Renewal, Brother Dylan. Renewal. When you go back home, your friends and associates will hardly recognize you. You'll radiate peace." She released her grip on my right arm.

"I don't know . . ."

Peter put his hand on my shoulder, said, "Brother Dylan, you're about to expand your awareness and detach from the material world."

"Can't detach too much," I said. "House payments, car payments, you know."

"The universe provides," Laura said.

Looking around the pool in search of Julie, I saw her hugging Brother Thomas—belly-button to belly-button. On my way to her, a hand reached out and grasped my arm.

"Brother Dylan, it's nice to have you with us," Brother John said; the voice of Charlton Heston playing God.

"It's nice to be here." I lied.

"You're an advertising agency art director."

Nod.

"We could use some promotional assistance."

"Really?"

"Instead of hoeing potatoes."

"I'd like that," I said. The truth.

Nodding, Brother John turned to welcome another student.

On my way to Julie, I eased around Owen who was hitting on Maria, who said, "Hi, you're Dylan."

"Maria, right?" I extended my hand, tried to avoid looking directly at her pert, pointy breasts. Rather than shaking hands, she drew me into an intimate hug. "M-m-m-m-m," I moaned, without thinking.

"M-m-m-m-m," she replied.

"How'd you like your steamed vegetables?" I said, releasing her. The dumb question just rolled out of my mouth.

She laughed, said, "I'm a masseuse. I'd like to work on you."

"I'd like you to work on me."

Out of the corner of my eye, I noticed Julie gesturing for me to join her. "Hi honey," she said, when I arrived at her side. "Brother Thomas is telling me about some of the unannounced activities."

"Like dancing naked around a bonfire?" I said.

"That's a special highlight," he replied without a touch of irony, his eyes looking up and off to the left, remembering. "A week from Wednesday is the full moon."

"Why do we do that?" I asked.

"To celebrate being children of the earth. We're not angels. We're physical beings who depend upon the earth to feed and preserve us. We must breathe, eat, mate, and find warmth and protection."

Julie, head bobbing in agreement, interrupted. "Brother Thomas just told me that Adam and Eve's desire for clothing is a metaphor for the materialistic desires that burden us down."

"I don't feel burdened."

Brother Thomas laid his hand on my shoulder. "Brother Dylan . . . your house payment, car payment, obligations, chaotic schedule?" He met my eyes, awaiting a response.

"Restaurants, television, rock-n'-roll, the Lakers," I said.

Face sad, he backed away until his upper arm rested against my wife's left breast. "I sense spirituality bubbling up within you, Brother Dylan. Within two weeks you'll be a changed man."

Beyond Julie one of the gay men stood alone at the far end of the pool. He waved. "Someone wants to talk to me," I said, moving away toward Daniel, a Don Johnson look-like.

"I sense a fish out of water," Daniel extended his hand. "Or maybe a fish in hot water."

I laughed. "Everybody else is into it, whatever it is."

Daniel shook his head. "Troy loves it, so I support him by coming along. Want some advice? The worst thing you can do is resist your wife's spiritual quest. She's in the true-believer, convert stage, and if you're smart you'll go along, tweaking her rudder, so to speak."

"I wouldn't know where to tweak."

Daniel drew me closer, lowered his voice. "Brother John combined psychiatry, Zen, Druidry, Wicca, and a little est to create his religion. A bit schitzy, but it makes as much sense as any other religion, if you're so inclined."

"Dancing around a bonfire?"

"That's just an excuse to have sex in the bushes."

"Huh?"

"You and your wife, or you can switch with another couple."

Primitive images danced in my mind, making it difficult to find words. "Thanks, Danie . . . er, Brother Daniel."

"Don't have to Brother me, but your wife will love the Sister bit."

## 6

"I don't believe how you've changed," Julie said, on the eleventh day of the retreat.

I responded with a blissful smile. I didn't feel changed, but I was flowing. Instead of hoeing potatoes, each afternoon I advised Brother John on how to advertise and promote The Brotherhood of Mystic Insight. Participation in sitting meditation, at first a painful bore, had become an opportunity to mentally explore business potentials — religious business potentials. Adapting to getting up at four in the morning wasn't difficult. Although I dreamed of eating a steak, my body seemed to thrive on gruel, steamed vegetables and black bread.

What I resisted most was Julie's enchantment with Brother Thomas, but I kept this to myself. Then on Tuesday of the second week, things came to a head in the processing session that followed Brother John's dharma talk.

"What do you most fear, Dylan?" As he spoke, Brother John stared out the wall of windows at Mt. Shasta. I glanced from Julie sitting beside me in a meditation posture to the other students watching me. Opening my mouth to speak, no words came out.

Brother John turned, met my eyes. "You are here to attain awareness, are you not?"

Fear slithered through my mental corridors looking for someplace to hide. Perspiration filmed my brow.

He waited.

"I fear my wife will be unfaithful."

"Dylan?" There was genuine surprise in Julie's voice.

Brother John tucked his fingers into the belt of his grey robe. "What about death, disease, poverty, war?"

"Of course, but infidelity somehow seems more immediate."

"You don't love your wife unconditionally."

"I do."

Brother John shook his head. "If you loved her unconditionally, and she desired to be with someone else, you would encourage her to find joy in the experience."

"Dylan's my husband. I have no desire to be with anyone else," Julie said.

I took her hand and squeezed. "Don't restraint and loyalty to our marriage vows have anything to do with it?"

Brother John ignored the question. "What is the very worst that would happen if Julie made love to another man?" He stood directly in front of me.

"That she would fall in love with him and leave me." I felt my face flushing and avoided Julie's eyes.

Brother John applied his Zen stare. The look was calculated to make us nervous and chatter on to avoid the silence.

It worked.

"That's it except"—I looked up at my spiritual teacher—"if Julie were to get pregnant by the other man . . ."

My energy drained away with the words, leaving me unprepared for further responses. For eleven days we'd been sitting in a semicircle meditating and being enlightened by Brother John. "What is your worst fear?" Four of the others had already run the gamut of endless questions. Lauren had feared Alzheimer's disease, which had claimed both her parents. Peter had feared his company would not survive another economic downturn. Mary had feared for her eleven-year-old son who had an irregular heartbeat. Holly had feared her family would find out she was a lesbian.

"How could you face your fear, Dylan?"

"What do you mean?"

"Courage is the willingness to be afraid and act anyway. You rise above the effects of your fears by facing them down."

"Are you telling me to have Julie make love to another man?"

"I'm asking, not telling."

"The only way I can think of facing the fear of my wife having sex with another man, is to ask her to have sex with another man." Chills scurried up my arms. Good Lord! The logic of his reasoning was escaping me, until I remembered Holly deciding to face her fear by calling her parents and explaining that her female roommate was her lover. The next day she said the world had lifted from her shoulders.

"Brother John, this is not something I worry about regularly. The fact is, I don't have many worries. It was the first thing that came into my mind." I glanced at Julie. She was looking at the floor.

Brother John waited.

I waited.

Finally, Julie raised her head, said, "Don't I have a little to say in this?" She looked from me to Brother John. "Dylan and I have been happily married for thirteen years. In that time, there have been numerous opportunities for affairs, but I've never even been seriously tempted."

"Julie is the best thing that ever happened to me," I said, more to my wife than anyone else.

My wife smiled and stared past Brother John, out the windows. I wanted to say more, to tell them all how I valued Julie's gentle way of being, her kind heart, and her intense sexuality. But instead, I silently waited for the storm to blow over.

"You could share the experience with your wife, Dylan."

"What?"

Then Brother John raised his arms in the air and said, "Everyone close your eyes and center yourself."

Releasing Julie's hand, I adjusted my position on the meditation pillow, straightened my back, and began to breathe deeply. Then as if everyone in the room were responding to some unheard cue, we all began to intone the "Aum" — the holy sound of earth-bound seekers communing with God. The undulating tones caressed my mind in gentle waves.

"Be aware that you are the center of your universe." Brother John's voice seemed far away. "You are all-knowing and all-powerful. All you need, all the knowledge you desire, lies within. All you have to do is be willing to receive. Whatever your situation or problem, you have the answers. You must simply learn to ask the right questions. Discovering the right questions is much more difficult than finding the right answers. And in search of those answers, I'm now going to ask you questions that are to be answered silently in your mind. Be honest with yourself, and trust the first thought that comes to you." He paused to let the words sink in. "What is the most important thing you would like to get handled now?"

There was no hesitation. It was as if my mind had a voice of its own: To rise above my jealous anxiety over the possibility of Julie's infidelity.

Brother John continued. "See the situation in your mind, the way it is now."

Instantly, my mind replayed the first night at the center, Julie naked in the spa, hugging Brother Thomas. But now she was kissing him, tenderly, then passionately. I was furious, screaming, chasing them as they ran hand-in-hand from the spa to the bushes.

"All right, now let's look at the situation the way you want it to be. Form a mental picture of the way you want it to turn out."

Images flickered within. Julie and I, white-haired, rocking side by side on a porch. Drawing back, I visualized a lush landscaped estate — the ultimate retirement palace. We made it, I thought. But within moments, another picture began to edge its way into the pastoral scene. I was exiting the front door of our home, locking an outside padlock — turning to see Julie waving goodbye from behind barred windows. I shuddered.

Brother John said, "What would you have to know, that you don't already know, that would allow this area of your life to clear up?"

The question fluttered through my mind like a drunken butterfly. I was still dealing with the visualization of locking Julie in a chastity belt of a house. *What would I have to know that I don't already know, that would allow* ... Okay. What? That she could have sex with another man and not want to leave me? An endorsement from Good Housekeeping guaranteeing I was a great lover and provider? Maybe Julie could work as a high-price call girl for a few weeks, and if she came back after the experience, I'd feel secure enough to release my fear. I realized a smile was creeping across my face. Chill out, Dylan.

Brother John said, "If you're stuck on this, you're choosing not to know something. You don't believe it is safe for you to be unstuck. That being the case, it's time to ask yourself the right questions."

Rise above your fear. Rise above your fear. Rise above your fear. The silent words reverberated like gun shots in a cavern. How? How? Do it. Do it. DO IT. What? The unthinkable. THE UNTHINKABLE.

Brother John said, "Good, are you willing to handle it?"

My eyes shot open. "Hell no!" I yelled, shooting to my feet. Momentarily unsteady, I waited for my legs to uncramp. Brother John reached out to touch my arm. I flinched, turned and bolted from the room.

# 7

"You okay?" Julie said, entering our cubicle.

Lying on my bunk, breathing deeply to calm down, I said, "Sorry. I'm sure Brother John thinks I'm an unevolved idiot."

"That's not important, Dylan."

I silently agreed.

She stretched, then sat on the edge of my bunk. "What's important is the fear behind your outburst."

"How do we get rid of it?" I asked.

Shrug. "Do you fear me enjoying another man sexually, or do you fear losing me as a result?"

"Losing you. I like you to enjoy yourself." But maybe not sexually with another man, I thought. "What if I were to make love to another woman? Would it upset you?"

"I don't think so, if you were honest about it. Some claim that exclusive coupling leads to boredom and possessiveness. But I've never been bored by our sex life."

"Neither have I, but I seem to be a bit possessive. Do you want to have sex with Brother Thomas?"

"It would be a nice treat, but it's not something I need to do."

"A nice treat?"

"I'd never act without your permission. Neither would he. Bad karma."

"What if I asked you to have sex with him tomorrow night as part of the bonfire ritual?"

"I'd say okay and tell you to do the same with one of the women."

"Really?"

"Really."

"In the bushes?"

"They tell me that's the tradition."

"Sister Maria's cute," I said. "The green-eyed brunette."

"I know who she is," Julie laughed. "We're friends. Want me to set it up?"

* * * * *

Illuminated by the full moon shining in the window of our cubicle, Julie smiled up at me from the bottom bunk when I stepped in the door.

"How was it?" I asked.

"Very nice, but not very comfortable in the grass." She grinned ear to ear.

Scratching myself, I said, "No poison ivy, I hope."

"Safe sex?" she asked.

I nodded. "You too?"

"Have we become pagans?"

"Did we really do what we did, Sister Julie?"

"Did Sister Maria have a good time?"

"Seemed to. What about Brother Thomas?"

"You're not jealous?"

"More turned on than jealous," I said, taking off my robe.

"I see," she said. "Bring that over here."

# 8

The following morning, Brother John talked about the Six Paramitas of the Boddhisattva. "According to these Zen Buddhist teachings, the person having sex with another must consider his own happiness, that of his companion and of the third person who will be most affected by his actions. If these three concerned people can be satisfied, then the sex act comes under natural law and is completely acceptable."

The dharma talk was followed by a group discussion. I apologized to the group for my previous outburst and said, "I think the bonfire romp was a wonderful experience, and I feel no jealousy. To the contrary, I feel an incredible sense of freedom."

"Why is that?" asked on of the participants.

"I faced my fear and survived. In fact, I enjoyed Julie's enjoyment."

Applause.

"You also faced and *enjoyed* Sister Maria," said someone else.

Laughter.

\* \* \* \* \*

At the end of our stay on Mt. Shasta, Brother John offered me a position as advertising/marketing director of the Brotherhood of Mystic Insight. I thought he was joking.

"We'll match your current salary. You, Julie and the children can live here rent free. Accumulate a nest egg."

"Oh, I don't think we could . . ."

"New bonfire ritual every two weeks," he added.

\* \* \* \* \*

Surprisingly, it took me a while to convince Julie.

"Why do I think it's sex, not spirituality, that's responsible for your conversion?" she asked.

"Blake said, 'Indulgence leads to the palace of wisdom.'"

That was two years ago—before my advertising ploys doubled the retreat enrollments at the center, before I started to channel, before Julie and I used our nest egg to start our own center in an old Girl Scout camp on Mt. Shasta. As a channeler, many women come to me for private counseling and individual blessings. Julie isn't as supportive as she used to be. Last week, as we drove past the golden arches, she wondered aloud about the taste of a hamburger.

I explained that she was being tempted by the dark forces and we meditated together to help her find the strength to remain strong. Then over a cup of herbal tea, we recalled the day Julie ran over Rufus—the family tragedy that had opened the door to our spiritual awakening.

# The Raffle

To raise money, Jennifer McGee decided to raffle off her husband in his next life. The flyer read:

*Murphy McGee*
*Raffle!*

*As a handsome, spiritual man, Murphy is bound to incarnate in his next life under more favorable circumstances than he experiences today. The winner of the raffle will be fated to mate with Murphy in his next incarnation. Tickets: $10.00 each. The drawing will be held at 3:00 PM in Booth 132, at the Mind, Body, Spirit Exposition on August 21. Exposition dates, location, and details on back.*

Murphy read the yellow flyer for the third time, folded it and slipped it into his T-shirt pocket. "I like the 'fated to mate' line, but how're you gonna guarantee they'll get me next go round, Jenny?"

"We'll use some tan-in-a-bottle stuff. Make you look more desirable. Tight jeans. Losing ten pounds wouldn't hurt, you know."

"Jen?"

"We need money, Murphy. Got any better ideas?"

"But—"

"There are lots of New Age women on the hunt." Jennifer kneeled over a blue cloth banner on the dining room floor. She dipped her brush in purple paint and carefully outlined the word IN. Murphy took interest in the way her buttocks listed from side to side in response to the angle of the brush strokes. The banner would run the width of the exposition booth and stated: <u>Assure Yourself A Soulmate In Your Next Life By</u>

Winning Murphy In This Life.

"Dumbest thing I've ever heard of."

"Five hundred tickets at $10 each. Nothing dumb about five grand, Murphy."

"I still don't understand how you can guarantee—"

The phone rang.

Murphy padded into the living room, picking up the cordless.

"Murphy McGee?" Without pausing for confirmation, the caller continued, "I'm Danny Bray at Fox-TV, have you ever seen my *Good Morning* show?"

"My favorite was the show when Shania Twain sang 'The Woman In'—"

"I'd like to have you and your wife on the Wednesday morning show."

"Neither of us can sing."

"You're being auctioned off this weekend, right?"

"Yeah, my wife, well—"

"Our viewers will love it. My producer will call you in a half hour."

There was a click on the other end of the line.

"Who wants to know if we can sing?" asked Jennifer.

"We're going to be celebrities," Murphy said, running fingers through his blond hair, which he wore short to minimize the roundness of his face. Who came to this conclusion wasn't clear, but Jennifer knew it wasn't Murphy. She considered his eyes his outstanding feature— wide baby-blues that looked perpetually surprised.

Red-haired, green-eyed Jennifer, stereotypically Irish in appearance, matched her husband's height, but unlike him, had managed to maintain her ideal weight according to the actuarial charts. Murphy had been one of Mountain Mutual's star insurance salesmen for fourteen years, but when it came to selling, he knew he couldn't hold a candle to his wife.

\* \* \* \* \*

"You'll be taken from the greenroom to the studio in about thirty minutes," said the young production assistant who looked disturbingly like Hillary Clinton must have looked two decades ago. She opened the door and ushered the McGees into the waiting room. Couches and chairs circled a large coffee table covered with boxes of doughnuts and bagels. Coffee urns sat on a table along the wall. Two TV monitors hung from the ceiling. On screen, Danny Bray interviewed the author of *Satan's Rainbow*.

"The New Age is in actuality an old ploy of the devil," said the author, a florid-faced man with thick glasses. He cupped his hand into a claw and squinted tiny eyes at the camera. Murphy wondered if the lights reflecting on the man's bald head cast a subliminal message of illumination or of a hothead. He chuckled at his unspoken assessment and chewed a doughnut.

Jennifer sipped coffee and scowled at the monitor. "He's talking about people like us, Murphy."

"Conflict programming generates viewer interest."

Jennifer recalled Geraldo's conflict programming—the fights, somebody hitting somebody with a chair. She shuddered. "Danny Bray's going to bait us with this guy."

"Be a Buddha," said Murphy.

The response wasn't what Jennifer expected. Just when she thought none of her metaphysics was sticking to Murphy, he came up with the right reply. They had been married sixteen years, but it wasn't until two years ago that she began to wonder if there wasn't more to life than she was experiencing. Her search ended with the discovery of the New Age movement.

Murphy didn't share the intensity of his wife's quest, but he figured reincarnation was more fun than Mass. He had been hypnotically regressed three times to discover incarnations as a Roman centurion, an American pilgrim, and a dance-hall whore during the California Gold Rush.

Murphy resisted the female incarnation.

"You have to experience both sexes and all races to round out your soul," Jennifer had explained.

"At least it shows I didn't make up the lifetime," he said.

"That which you resist, you become. Resist being a woman, next life you'll become one."

"Give me a break."

"A Universal law."

That ended that. Murphy preferred not to know more.

On the greenroom TV monitors, Danny Bray asked the author what he thought about the Mind, Body, Spirit Exposition to be held next weekend at the civic auditorium.

"S-S-S-SATAN'S LAIR," he hissed, mouth distorting, eyes narrowing to peepholes.

"Well . . ." Danny Bray looked directly into the camera, raised his index finger and said, "Our next guests are a couple who will not only attend the festival, the wife is going to raffle off her husband in his next life. We'll be right back after this commercial break."

The young Hillary led Jennifer and Murphy though a maze of hallways to the *Good Morning Show* set. Bray didn't look up from his notes as his guests were directed to the interview couch. Murphy sat next to the host's desk, Jennifer in the middle, the author to her right. A sound engineer clipped tiny microphones to Murphy's shirt and Jennifer's sweater. Murphy smiled at the author who scowled in response. Beyond the lights and cameras, sat an audience of 100 people.

A commercial for Baby Ruth® candy bars played on the monitor, while young women in Fox-TV uniforms passed out free samples to the studio audience. "Hype them up with a sugar rush," Jennifer whispered to Murphy. Murphy accepted two candy bars. He ate one during the newsbreak.

A tall man wearing a headset yelled, "Ten seconds." He counted down by flicking his fingers in the air: five, four, three, two, one.

"And welcome back." Danny Bray provided a one-paragraph background introduction for the McGees, then said, "Jennifer, how can you raffle off Murphy in his next incarnation?"

"A MOCKERY OF GOD'S COMMANDMENTS!" yowled the author.

Jennifer turned to the man and said, "What commandment? Thou shalt not raffle thy husband?" The audience laughed appreciatively.

The author shivered, twitched, knitted his hands.

Bray said, "Now, now, everyone has a right to their own beliefs." He looked at Jennifer, waiting for her answer.

"Tickets are $10. On the last day of the Expo, we draw a winner and perform a unity ritual at Booth 132."

"WITCHCRAFT!"

Bray ignored the author. "What's a unity ritual?"

"A marriage ceremony that is projected into the future."

"Sounds complicated." Bray turned to the author. "Any comments?"

"LORD OF THE FLIES!" The author's voice, already shrill and whiny, reached a level that could break glass. "HARLOT!" Trembling, he edged away from Jennifer. "WARLOCK!" he squealed at Murphy.

"DIPSHIT!" Murphy yelled back.

Danny Bray threw up his arms, said, "Mr. McGee, we cannot have that kind of language on this—"

"OH-O—O-O-O-O! GOD SAVE ME FROM THESE VERMIN!" The author quivered, twitched, and clenched his eyes shut.

Murphy's face flushed, a bead of sweat rolled down his cheek. "Harlot? Vermin?" He reached over his wife, grabbed the author's necktie with his left hand, and drove his fist into the man's nose. The microphone on Jennifer's sweater amplified the sound of breaking bone.

"OW-O-O-O-O-O-O-O!"

"BE A BUDDHA, MURPHY!" Jennifer was covered with blood. "COMMERCIAL BREAK!" shrieked Danny Bray.

A close-up of a toilet bowl cleaner appeared on the monitors. There was a momentary pause before Bray turned to Murphy. "YOU NEW AGE NITWIT, WHAT DO THINK YOU'RE DOING?"

Beyond the cameras, a middle-aged female producer shrieked at the ceiling, but couldn't be heard over Bray's rant. A few people in the audience were cheering, others booing. Out of the corner of her eye, Jennifer saw a white-haired woman clobber a man with her handbag. A skinhead leaped out of the audience and back-handed the wailing author. When a cameraman raced to the author's assistance, someone hit him from behind.

Bray was leaning over his desk, lifting Murphy off the couch by his lapels when someone from the audience began shaking the scenic backdrop. Murphy looked up to see it teetering. As the wooden wall tipped toward him, he wrenched free of Bray's grasp, grabbed Jennifer and dove to the floor. The structure collapsed on Danny Bray in an explosion of splintering wood.

"Oh-o-o-o-o-o!"

On their hands and knees, Jennifer and Murphy crawled out from under the rubble in the direction of the audience. Beyond the brawling people, a uniformed guard was racing down the aisle toward the me-lee on the set. Several people were trying to rescue Bray. Others were fighting. More were screaming. Two cameras had been knocked over by the falling wall, and a severed electrical cable sparked and slithered like a berserk reptile.

"Guess the interview's over." Murphy stood, helped his wife to her feet and began to brush the dust and debris from his clothes.

"Let's go home, Buddha."

\* \* \* \* \*

The "Fox event" was the talk of the town. To some of those of a metaphysical persuasion, Murphy became a New Age John Wayne. To other New Agers, Murphy had created some bad karma. To people who had never thought about a New Age, the weekend Expo sounded wonderfully volatile — a little like a hockey game — one minute skating, the next an all-out brawl.

The publicity generated the largest attendance in Mind, Body, Spirit history.

And then there was the raffle.

By 3:00 PM Sunday afternoon, 1,723 women had purchased a raffle ticket. Everyone wanted to personally congratulate Murphy on putting the author in his place, even if it wasn't a very spiritual way to handle conflict. The actual drawing had to be held onstage in the convention-center auditorium. All local TV stations covered the ceremony.

A 44-year-old schoolteacher named Natalie won Murphy. The couple-to-be was married by Jennifer within a circle of 24 chanting, hand-holding New Agers. Music was provided by a trio playing the tambourine, flute and tin whistle. To clinch the future union everyone onstage and in the audience visualized the couple happily united in their next incarnation.

When it was over, Natalie asked Jennifer if she could take Murphy home for the evening, "To sample the merchandise, so to speak."

Jennifer refused.

The money amounted to $17,230 minus the cost of the booth. On the way home, Murphy said, "They have these Expos in cities all over the country. Let's raffle you off in New York next month."

# Childhood Hero

"People who live as if there were no hereafter, cross over into the lower astral planes when they die. Call it a waiting place, call it purgatory, call it the abyss — whatever you call it, the fact remains that the lower astral represents a repugnant confusion to the jaded, a maze of horrors to the damned, and a nightmare to the suicides," I said, shuddering. "For here in the infernal mist, lost souls wander in unending confusion and fear. For them, for awhile, often a long while, they exist to experience the manifestations of their own demented minds."

The woman, sitting at the other end of the couch, nodded her head. Stern-looking, her short dark hair framed an ashen face. Early forties. She was dressed in a navy blue wool suit. In addition to taping the interview, she also made notes in a leather-bound book.

Warm afternoon sunlight filtered through the blinds into the office, illuminating framed degrees hanging on the wall. The thought of putting my feet up on the teakwood coffee table crossed my mind but I decided it would not convey the proper image.

I sipped my coffee, then said, "It's very important that you do not omit any details. I'm willing to share it, but I don't want anyone to misunderstand."

She nodded and smiled. "I realize how important it is to you." Her voice was surprisingly soft and understanding.

"Let me begin at the beginning. Did you have a childhood hero?" I asked. The woman nodded.

I continued. "People usually choose role models while in the early years of high school. This hero could be someone in school, a family member, a public figure . . . anyone. You start to imitate them without realizing it. The role model then becomes incorporated into your self-image. You go through life making small decisions as if you were responding to individual circumstances. But the truth is, there's a master plan. You set it in motion when you chose your hero.

"My childhood hero was Trent Rainy, the great country singer. Remember? He died of a drug overdose in an Oklahoma City hotel in 1955. In high school I lived for his music—worked as a bag boy in a grocery store to get the money to buy his records. When he made a personal appearance in Omaha, I waited five hours in a rainstorm to be the first person into that auditorium. Front row center. Then for two hours he sang all those wonderful songs about woes I'd never experienced. After the show I got his autograph in a little book I'd purchased just for the occasion."

A thermal pot of coffee sat on the coffee table. I opened the top and offered to refill the woman's cup. She shook her head. Refilling my own, I savored the rich, steamy aroma.

"What happened next?" she asked.

"After Trent died, I still loved his music. I wore out all the old 45s, but then they rereleased the songs on cassettes, and today, CDs are even better. Would you like to hear one?"

She shook her head. "Maybe later."

"Anyway, then in the 1970s, I became interested in the occult and studied Edgar Cayce, took ESP classes, learned astral projection."

"Did you get involved in drugs?" she asked.

"No more than anyone else," I said.

"How many times was Trent Rainy married?"

"Three times."

"And you were married three times?"

"Yes. But that's not relevant to the story."

"The background is always relevant to the story," she said, making more notes.

"This story is about me deciding to meet my childhood hero in 1976," I said.

"But I thought Trent Rainy was dead."

"While in my astral body, I could slip through the veil to the other side and seek him out."

"How do you do that?" she asked.

"I have every song Trent ever recorded, videotapes of his appearances on the 'Grand Ole Opry,' and audio recordings of all his interviews. I've read every book ever written about him. I even have three scrapbooks of newspaper clippings and magazine stories. I know him in here." I placed my hand on my heart.

She was about to ask another question, but I continued. "You see, everyone has a unique vibrational tone. I know Trent Rainy so well, I can capture his essence in my mind. So that's exactly what I did. After twelve hours of listening to his music, watching the videos and reading the scrapbooks, I went into hypnosis and left my body. Then I condensed my awareness, matched his vibrational tone and shot off in search of him on the other side."

"The other side?"

"The astral planes. There are seven primary levels, more levels within those primary levels. The first level is the lower astral." I looked at her and she nodded. "The top level, the seventh, is the Godhead."

"And you visited these levels while out of your body? While astral projecting?" she asked.

"The second and third levels. The vibrations of the higher levels were too intense to penetrate. I tried several times, but didn't succeed."

"And the lowest level?" she asked.

"I had always been able to ascend right through the lower astral planes, until I went looking for Trent Rainy, that is." I rubbed my arms to quell the tingling goosebumps.

"Focusing on Trent Rainy's essence sucked me right into a nightmare. Twisting and tumbling through that gray mist, even my astral body shivered in the godawful cold. Then I landed. Not on my feet, but in a tumbling roll that carried me over the edge of a path and down an incline through the sludge into dead brush. I'll never forget looking up through the leafless branches into that iridescent gray mist. There was a hum. It was an unearthly, almost expectant sound.

"Trying to wipe off the stinking mud, I stood up and looked around, my eyes beginning to penetrate the mist. I don't know how to describe what I saw. Imagine a barren, devastated landscape—an area blackened and blasted as if by fire, or a nuclear holocaust. The ground was a mixture of grit, slush and mud, and the trees and bushes were nothing but skeletal silhouettes against that eerie light. And it was still, like a vacuum. An absence of air, color and life."

"You called it purgatory?" the woman said.

"Maybe. Maybe the Catholic Church learned about it the same way I did and decided to incorporate it into their doctrine," I replied.

She tapped her pen on her notepad and said, "According to the Catholic Church, purgatory is a place where souls are purified from excusable sins, or where they undergo their remaining temporal punishment."

I nodded.

"Are you religious?" she asked.

"I pray fervently."

"Did you find Trent Rainy?"

"Oh, yes. After the angel found me."

"The angel?"

"I assumed he was an angel. He was standing on the path above me—a middle-aged man dressed in white. He smiled at me and asked, 'Why are you here?' I climbed back up to the path and explained that I was trying to find Trent Rainy."

"'The living don't belong here,' he said. 'You'll see things beyond your ability to accept.'

"'But why are you here?' I asked.

"'Slum work,' he said. 'I'm from the fourth level. I serve by trying to convince lost souls to follow me to the light.'

"'Why wouldn't they?' I asked, looking around me. 'Who would want to stay here?'

"'Those who are so confused as to know no better,' he said. 'Those whose anger blocks reason. Those whose hatred obscures common sense. Those whose addictions veil liberation. Trent Rainy is at the bottom of the hill.' He pointed down the path.

"'Has he been here for thirty-six years?' I asked.

"'A short time for many,' the angel replied as he disappeared. 'Good luck,' said a voice in the mist.

"Trent Rainy was sitting on the stump of a tree at the bottom of the hill. I approached him cautiously.

"'Hey,' he called out to me. 'Got any uppers or downers?' His voice was deep and raspy and Southern. He licked his lips. 'Man, what I wouldn't do for some H.'

"He was hollow-eyed and ghostly-pale, but aside from that, Trent Rainy still looked twenty-nine. Now I was older than he, or at least I looked it.

"'I don't have any drugs,' I said. 'But I came to see you.'

"'No drugs?'

"'I was a fan of yours. You gave me your autograph when I was sixteen years old.'

"'Yeah?'

"'*Back Street Blues* has always been my favorite song.'

"'I usually close with that song. When I get the hell out of here I'll give you a pass.'

"'A pass?'

"'To the Opry. Problem is I need something to clear out the cobwebs, if you know what I mean.' His hands shook and he clasped them so I wouldn't notice. 'It's like the pain and shakes never go away, if you know what I mean.' He looked down at the ground and twisted the toe of a cowboy boot in the muck.

"'I think I know what you mean,' I said. 'Before you died, you were—'

"'Died? What the hell is wrong with you, man? Do I look dead? Now if you ask, do I *feel* like I'm dead, that's another story.' He chuckled. 'The road,' he said, 'the road wears you down, if you know what I mean. A different hotel every night. Horseshit food. Only thing I can't complain about is the women. I party every night with the cutest little tight-buns in the audience, if you know—'

"I interrupted, 'How long have you been here?'

"'Can't rightly say. Sometimes it feels like a long time, but when you're hurtin', time goes slow, if you know what I mean. I remember playing Oklahoma City, but then everything got kind of screwed up, if you—'

"'You're dead, Trent. I wish you weren't. I wish you could write and record some new songs but that just isn't going to happen.'

"He looked at me for a long time, then said, 'Listen, man, if you could just find me an upper or two, I could get the hell out of here, and I'd write you a song.'"

The woman set her coffee cup hard on the table, pulling me out of my reverie. "So you couldn't talk Trent into going to the light?"

"Well, I went to visit him, not save him. But when I fully understood his predicament, I decided how heroic it would be to save my childhood hero."

She smiled.

"So I started visiting him regularly. That's how I learned so much about the lower astral planes. Of course, the visits took their toll."

"Your wife left you?" the interviewer asked.

"You know about that? Well, she didn't like me coming back in a cold sweat, trembling, crying about what I'd seen, praying for God to forgive my sins so I wouldn't get stuck in that terrible place." My whole body shook so badly I had to put down my coffee cup. "Loathsome, vile, rotten—you can't imagine. No one can."

The woman flipped back through the pages in her leather notebook. "Your ex-wife says she begged you to stop astral projecting."

"You talked to Susan?"

"Of course," the interviewer said. "I need to know the whole story."

"I had to save Trent Rainy. It became an obsession."

"You lost your job?"

"Yes, after Susan left. But I was making headway with Trent Rainy. He remembered me between visits. Finally, eight months and a hundred astral projections later, Trent went to the light." I laughed.

"And you started using uppers and downers. Heroin, too, according to a police report."

"Well, it was a hard time, if you know what I mean. But he was my hero, I had to—"

There was a knock on the door.

"Come in," the woman said.

"Doctor, I'm sorry to interrupt, but you have an emergency call on line three."

"That's all right. We were just wrapping up today's session." She turned to me, patted me on the knee and said, "We'll talk again at the same time next Thursday."

I stood up and the nurse took my arm. As we walked out of the office, she turned to address the doctor. "The usual sedative?"

"Yes," the doctor said as the door closed.

Arm in arm, the nurse and I walked slowly down the hospital corridor. "Did you have a childhood hero?" I asked.

# The Woman Who Visited Psychics

The aromas of freshly brewed coffee and fried bacon lingered in the air as Naomi Wainwright sat at the breakfast table watching her husband Robert thumb through his newspaper. Even reading the *Los Angeles Times,* he projected a lawyerly detachment. Six feet tall and of average build, he retained a full head of graying hair and maintained a golf-course tan.

Between each sip of coffee, Naomi took a deep breath and sighed.

"You all right, dear?" Robert said without looking up.

"I'm going to die at forty-five." The words rolled off her lips with the finality of the incoming tide.

"You've been saying that for fifteen years." Robert spread orange marmalade on his English muffin.

"And now I'm forty-four." She idly rolled her locket between her thumb and index finger. The 24-carat gold heart contained a picture of her three grown children.

"No one knows when they're going to die, Naomi."

"You'll be saying that over my coffin." She reached across the table for the marmalade.

"Naomi, quit. For God's sake, quit." Robert folded his newspaper and looked up, his gaze skipping over his wife to the backyard swimming pool. The automatic skimmer crisscrossed the surface of the water like a giant spider. The palm trees surrounding the pool quivered in the rippling air.

"I've heard about a new psychic in the Palisades. Actresses use her to guide their careers."

"That's nice, dear."

"Maybe she can save me."

"I hope she makes you feel better."

"I have an appointment today at eleven."

"That's nice."

"Will you be home by six?"

He nodded, kissed her on the cheek, and was gone.

Alone at the table, Naomi stacked dirty dishes and thought about dying. At night, when sleep wouldn't come, she fantasized her funeral in vivid detail: the flowers, the songs, her children's tearful goodbyes, the assembled mourners. She could not imagine seeing herself in a casket, so she closed the coffin and placed her favorite photograph upon the lid—the one with her in the red bathing suit.

"Mom, you look just like Marilyn Monroe," her daughter Julie said, on seeing the photo ten years before.

She still had the same blonde hair thanks to Derrick at the Beauty Secret. Sure, she carried 20 extra pounds, but so did her friends. The facial wrinkles running from her nose down to the edge of her mouth were getting deeper. She'd have a facelift if she were going to live longer.

At night, her dreams often followed a painful course from the funeral to Robert the widower being pursued by scheming Beverly Hills women—some of them her friends, for God's sake! They invited him to dinner, to the theater, to Aspen for a skiing weekend. Invariably, she awakened filled with anxiety and scowling in disgust at her sleeping husband.

Traffic was sparse on Sunset Boulevard as Naomi eased her Mercedes E320 into the winding curves, through Brentwood to Pacific Palisades where the road curved out of the hills and swept down to disappear into the fog on Pacific Coast Highway.

The address was a mobile home park a hundred yards above the beach, terraced to offer a view of Santa Monica Bay when the fog burned away or was blown back out to sea.

Naomi parked beside a new Jaguar. As upper crust as one can

get and live in a trailer, she thought. President Reagan had once lived a few miles away. She wondered if Nancy consulted Madam Grissel.

The door opened before Naomi knocked. The scent of incense and candle wax wafted out of the dark doorway. "Naomi Wainwright, come in, come in."

"Madam Grissel. I've heard so much about you."

The psychic was about Naomi's age with ebony hair piled high on her head, sprouting ringlets that fell over her chipmunk cheeks. Her heavily made-up eyes had oriental folds, although she did not look Asian. Her lips were thin: a ruby line. She was dressed in a flower-print Hawaiian muumuu.

"Please, sit down." The psychic pointed to an overstuffed couch along the wall, the only seating in the room. "Would you like a cup of tea?"

"Thank you."

Eyes slowly adjusting to the darkness, Naomi squinted into the shadowed room. Black curtains covered the windows. A brass floor lamp with a fringed parchment shade cast an eerie light over the large pentagram painted on the floor. Unlit white candles, nearly buried in mounds of melted wax, sat at each of the five points of the star.

"How did you hear about me?" Madam Grissel asked, handing Naomi a cup of herbal tea. The psychic sat on the couch beside her client.

The tea released a bouquet of spice and something Naomi couldn't quite place. *Mold?* Looking over the top of the cup, she said, "My masseuse at the Sports Connection told me you've guided Mandy Adams' acting career."

Madam Grissel nodded. "Have you been to many psychics?"

"Yes, many."

"Are they accurate?"

"Sometimes, about some things."

"I am always accurate about everything. That's why I charge what I do."

"Three hundred, is that correct?" Naomi drew the bills from her purse, handed them to the psychic.

"Did your masseuse tell you how I work?"

Naomi shook her head, sipped the tea.

"All right, we begin by having you take off all your clothes and removing your jewelry."

"Naked?"

"You must lie nude within the pentagram, your head facing north."

Still shaking her head, Naomi stood up. "I'm not interested in black magic."

Madam Grissel remained sitting, knees together, holding the saucer in one hand, teacup in the other. "Neither am I, Mrs. Wainwright. This is how I will obtain the answers you desire, including information about your forthcoming death."

"You know about *that*?"

"Nudity in magic is simply part of the ritual. It is very spiritual." The psychic smiled.

"What will happen?"

Pointing to the pentagram, Madam Grissel said, "You'll lie with your head within the top point, your arms extended into the upper points, and your legs within the lower points. I'll light the candles and will sit outside the circle at your head. When I go into trance my control takes over."

"Control?"

"A contact in spirit named Rashanda. He'll speak through me, directly to you." Madam Grissel slipped the muumuu off over her head, to stand naked before her client. Naomi couldn't help staring. Tattooed upon her 44E breasts were faces. On the left a smiling face, on the right, a sad face. Her nipples served as noses.

The psychic waddled to the top point of the pentagram and kneeled down as if in church. Lighting the candle, she said, "I exorcise thee, O creature of wax, by Him who alone hath created all things by His word."

Naomi noticed that as the psychic performed the ritual, raising and lowering her arms, the faces on her breasts changed expression. Lighting a candle at each point of the pentagram, Madam Grissel chanted, calling upon unseen angels to protect her. The smell of candle wax filled the small room. Naomi's mind reeled at the absurdity of the situation, but she found herself feeling euphoric as she unbuttoned her blouse.

Madam Grissel kneeled prayerfully in the center of the circle, surrounded by five flickering candles. She said, "When you can stand shamelessly before existence, with no secrets, with no privacy, the healing begins and miracles happen."

Naomi, now naked, shuddered, not knowing what to do with her hands.

The psychic continued. "You treat your body as a temple, Naomi, and it shows. Don't be embarrassed. You're beautiful. All nature is nude except man. Our clothes disconnect us from nature."

Madam Grissel stood, stepped out of the pentagram and gestured for her client to take her place. Naomi laid down on the cold floor. When she was as comfortable as she was going to get, she closed her eyes. The psychic began to hum the aum and chant an incantation calling down the power of powers and beseeching Rashanda to join her.

Breathing deeply, trying to relax, Naomi could feel the warmth of the candles on her fingers and toes. She wondered what her husband would say if he could see her now. Naomi, have you gone out of your ever-loving mind? No doubt about it. Maybe I have, she thought. Then she decided if Mandy Adams, the TV star of *House Husband* could lay naked in this pentagram, so could she. Nancy Reagan, on the other hand, was difficult to imagine. She decided the first lady did not consult Madam Grissel after all.

"I AM RASHANDA," boomed the voice above Naomi's head. It sounded male and a little like fingernails being drawn across a blackboard.

Naomi trembled.

"I have come to tell you of your past, present and future. So you will not doubt my validity, I will remind you of things only you recall. The game you played in your mother's broom closet at age thirteen, your experience with Jonathan in his parked car on Claxton Road, and the secret trip to Mexico in 1972."

Naomi tittered with embarrassment. "I accept your validity," she said.

"You fear you are going to die at forty-five."

Nod. "I've known my destiny for years."

"Because of the repetitive dream?" the voice asked.

"You know about that, too?"

"Of course."

Naomi released a prolonged sigh.

"Tell me of the dream."

"It's just that I'm forty-four now, and I know I'm going to die at forty-five. I don't want to leave the children."

"Yes."

"I try not to die, but I do anyway."

"That was in Italy in 1863."

"I don't understand."

"In that incarnation you raised orphan children who were dependent upon you. You resisted death because you feared what would happen to the children. The fear was so intense it scarred your soul, and you continue to carry that fear. Let go of it."

Naomi smiled. *I'm not going to die at forty-five?* she wondered.

"You are not going to die at forty-five," the voice said. "Your children in this life were some of the orphans in that life. Your husband in this life was a female friend in the Italian incarnation."

"Robert wouldn't accept that," Naomi whispered.

"He might if you first helped him to experience his feminine essence."

"What do you mean?"

"Use your imagination."

"What can you tell me about my future?"

"Until five minutes ago you did not accept the potential of a future. Now that you have one you can make of it what you will."

Naomi questioned Rashanda about her husband, her children, and her past lives, until the spirit said, "It is time for me to go. Thank Madam Grissel for me."

In response to a *woooshing* sound, Naomi opened her eyes. The candles were flickering as if in a draft. Madam Grissel moaned.

\* \* \* \* \*

Naomi was placing a casserole in the oven when Robert entered the kitchen from the attached garage. "I'm *not* going to die at forty-five, honey," she said, her voice joyous, expectant.

"I've been telling you that for fifteen years." He kissed her on the cheek on his way through the room.

When she heard him mixing his nightly martini at the bar in the living room, she joined him with a steaming mug in her hands.

"Robert, please don't drink that. Shasento tea will give you a lift, but a healthy lift."

Robert looked at her as if she were crazy. She set the cup on the bar. "It smells like moldy oranges," he said, the corners of his mouth turning down.

"You were my female friend in your last life," she said.

He dropped an olive into the martini.

"Do you accept that?" she said.

"If it makes you feel better, dear." He crossed the room, eased into his relax-o-lounger chair, punching buttons on a remote control. The television set flickered to life. Nightly news.

"Madam Grissel has comedy and tragedy faces tattooed on her breasts. Her nipples are the noses." Naomi stood beside the TV, cupping her breasts with her hands.

Robert looked at his wife with a blank expression.

"She made me lie naked on the floor in the middle of a pentagram."

"I don't think I need to know —"

"The spirit that channels through Madam Grissel says I should help you experience your feminine essence. So, I purchased rose quartz gemstones for you to sleep on." Smiling, she looked into her husband's eyes.

Robert met her gaze, took a long sip of the martini, scowled, and said, "Naomi, keep this up and you're going to die at forty-five."

# Time Heals All ...

After months of suffering, Helen Riley's husband of eleven years died of cancer. He was thirty-eight. Too young to leave life, to leave her. From the day of the initial diagnosis, Helen lived in denial. Mark could fight it, beat it. Become a statistical exception.

Radiation. Chemotherapy. The Greek treatment in Mexico was supposed to provide a miracle. But the malignancy spread from his lungs, to his bones, to his liver — an ever-expanding darkness on the X-rays.

"How long?"

"A month. Maybe a little more."

"There's nothing else we can do?"

"Why not take a cruise? The morphine will block most of your husband's pain."

But he wanted to die at home. Near the end, he became like a lovable three-year-old — lucid for brief periods, followed by long sleep. The sleep eventually turned into a coma. When he cried out in pain, Helen injected the morphine through a portal, directly into his heart — sometimes every ten minutes.

"Give him permission to die," Helen's mother said. "He's hanging on out of fear of leaving you."

So she whispered lies: "It's all right to let go, Mark. I understand."

When his breathing became a death rattle, she held him in her arms for an hour before his spirit left the body. She felt it go. The reality of that moment was not what she expected. *One moment I'm a wife, the next a widow. Just like that. Click. Somewhere in the statistical archives I've become a single woman. One less marriage. One less white male populating the planet. Click, click.* Later, she decided this reaction was a way of avoiding the real meaning of the horrible moment.

When the ambulance came, she couldn't watch them take him away.

She took a pill to sleep, but awakened in the middle of the night to see a light glowing at the foot of the bed.

"You're here, aren't you, Mark?"

Her mother stayed with her in the apartment for the first week. "You have to accept that he's gone, Helen."

"I can't."

"You have to."

"Never."

Helen read books about death, dying, and contacting the other side. Automatic writing would allow her to make direct contact with Mark. She practiced inducing an altered state of consciousness, practiced the writing technique according to the instructions on an audio tape: "When you open your eyes, just barely open them and begin writing. If your hand does not take off on its own, begin to make ovals across the page. This allows the energy to continue flowing through your physical body and mind, down to the paper. At first you may only receive a few words, but with every session, you'll receive more. The goal is total automatic writing—to set aside your ego and become a clear channel for the discarnate who directs your pen."

The first attempt resulted in four pages of ovals. Among the ovals on page three, she made out the word *love*—on page four, the word *you*. Discovering this message, her hands trembled.

"You're here, aren't you, Mark?"

Every morning, every evening, she induced an altered state and called upon Mark to direct her hand. On the fourth day, among pages of ovals, she made out the words, *I – was – called – to – the – light – Love – You.*

Twenty days after her first attempt, all the ovals had been replaced with words: *My Dearest Helen, I'm right here beside your chair, controlling the pen. I love you. I'll always love you. I can now move freely back and forth from my natural vibrational level to the physical plane. When you think of me, your thoughts are a voice within me. I feel your torment and send you soothing energy. I'll always be here when you need me, but you must go on with your life. Forever, Your Mark.*

Her tears fell upon the words, which ran together—a blue river across the notebook page. "Mark, I can't let you go."

Flipping the page, she wrote across the top of a clean sheet: TELL ME ABOUT THE OTHER SIDE AND HOW YOU CAN COME BACK TO ME. Then she closed her eyes, relaxed her body, and counted herself down while loosely holding the pen. She waited.

*My Dearest Helen, The other side is a wondrous place. When I died in your arms, I floated above our physical bodies and was shouting your name when my father arrived. He welcomed me and pointed out that my pain was gone. What a relief that was. My spirit guide—an Asian woman—explained that when I was ready, I could follow her to the light. During my morphine dreams, I had seen her nearby, waiting. Anyway, I wouldn't leave your side for several days. But after the funeral, my guide convinced me to go with her to the light. She said I could return to you soon.*

*The light was more or less an orientation process. I had to review my life and note areas requiring additional learning. That's not exactly accurate, but it's close.*

*I am just beginning to comprehend the process of my thoughts manifesting reality. If I want to live in a large ranch house like the one we dreamed of building, I have only to think of the house and it appears. Once I learned how to do it, I tried to manifest you, but it didn't work. Only when you're out of body, astral projecting, can we be together over here.*

*In regard to your last question, I want to come back to you more than I ever wanted anything while living on the earth. But I can't come back. Forever, Your Mark.*

That night while asleep, Helen walked up the steps of a familiar ranch house and found Mark in the living room. They embraced passionately, looked deep into each other's eyes, and he took her hand and led her upstairs. The bedroom furniture was right out of a *Sundance* catalog. The windows framed a snow-capped mountain range.

The orgasm awakened her. She was back in the apartment, gasping for breath, trembling atop sweat-soaked sheets.

MY DEAREST MARK, WHAT HAPPENED LAST NIGHT? YOUR HELEN

*My Dearest Helen, You came to me in your astral body—to our dream house. Remember how we used to describe it to each other? We had astral sex.*

*Not the same as on earth, but I'm not complaining. I miss you so. Forever, Your Mark.*

MY DEAREST MARK, I'M GOING TO TAKE A WEEK OF VACATION FROM WORK AND GO BACK EAST TO THE MONROE INSTITUTE FOR ASTRAL PROJECTION TRAINING. THAT WAY I CAN PROJECT TO YOU CONSCIOUSLY. YOUR HELEN.

*My Dearest Helen, It would be wonderful to have you consciously interacting with me again, but my guide says you must go on with your life. My death was karmic. I must study and perform service work over here, and you have a destiny to fulfill upon the earth. When you die naturally, we'll be together again. How I wish it could be otherwise. Forever, Your Mark.*

MY DEAREST MARK, TELL YOUR GUIDE THAT I LOVE YOU MORE THAN LIFE ITSELF, AND I WILL DO WHATEVER I HAVE TO DO TO BE WITH YOU.

Ten days later, Helen embraced her husband in his non-physical but form-oriented world. "This is better."

"You always were a determined woman," he said.

"At the institute, they taught me to leave my body at will. Takes just a few minutes." She held Mark's hand as they walked up the steps and into the ranch house.

An Asian woman was waiting in the living room. "Helen, you should not be doing this. You're keeping Mark from completing his transition."

Helen extended her hand in a gesture of friendship.

"I am Taroo, Mark's spirit guide."

"Yes," Helen said. "And I'd like to discuss walk-in potentials."

"Out of the question," Taroo said.

"What's going on?" Mark said.

"Mark, they could let your soul walk into the body of someone on earth who wants to die. Maybe someone whose life is so messed up they're contemplating suicide. When that person is out of body during sleep, an agreement could be struck between the two of you. They agree to leave their body, never to return, and without incurring any negative karma. You step into their body and agree to clean up their life, before pursuing your own agenda."

"How do you know this?" Mark said.

"I've read about it. Talked to walk-ins who have a Minnesota organization and their own newsletter."

Mark looked at Taroo.

"It can be done, but it isn't your plan," the woman said.

"But I want to be with Helen. Anything to be with—"

"If it isn't done, I will consciously astral-project to Mark until my earthly body gives out," Helen said.

"Unacceptable," Taroo said.

"Watch me."

"You can't direct the spiritual world from an earthly position, young lady."

"Taroo, you remind me of a nun who taught fourth grade at St. Sebastian's."

Mark took Helen's hand. "Ladies, please!"

\* \* \* \* \*

Helen asked for a one-month leave of absence from work. She told her mother and friends that she was going to Hawaii to get her head together. Then each morning in the apartment, she inserted ear plugs and drew a face mask over her eyes as she lay down in bed. Astral projection was easy now—five minutes from wide awake to lift out. The routine was to remain out on the astral plane for three hours, return, get up, eat, exercise, and then go back to Mark.

For the next three weeks she helped Mark decorate the ranch house. She'd describe a piece of furniture or an accessory, and he would manifest his interpretation of his wife's concept. Sometimes she'd laugh out loud at his creation and it often took him several attempts to create the item successfully.

About the time the house was finished, Taroo appeared with a white-haired man in a white robe.

"I understand you've joined us while still living on the earth plane," he said.

Helen extended her hand. "I'm Helen."

"Jonathan." He nodded, smiling. "Using thought forms to create reality helps newcomers adjust to these realms, but Mark has much more important work to do."

"I want Mark to walk-in."

"So I understand."

"You can arrange it."

"Our concern is establishing a precedent."

"I won't tell anyone."

"I doubt they would believe you if you did."

Helen smiled. "You've made a decision, haven't you?"

"We have three walk-in candidates. An 18-year-old gang member who knows he is marked for death. A 50-year-old ailing doctor, and a 45-year-old widower who refuses to adjust to the loss of his wife."

"We'll take the widower," Helen said.

Jonathan nodded. "His name is Victor Norris. You realize Mark would walk into Victor's body with Victor's memories intact. When you meet Mark as Victor, he won't consciously recognize you. But on a soul level he'll probably feel a strong attraction."

"Where does Victor live?" Helen asked.

"Des Moines, Iowa."

"Will Victor recall his life as Mark under hypnotic regression?"

"Probably."

\* \* \* \* \*

Helen researched Victor Norris—a stockbroker with two grown sons. His wife's death had sent him into a two-year depression from which he had been unable to emerge, until a month ago. Helen's private detective casually inquired about Victor with his colleagues.

"One day, he just seemed to come out of it. Just like that, he's enthusiastic about life again. Amazing isn't it?

"He went home from the office with a black cloud over his head and returned the next morning projecting sunshine. Nobody could believe it."

An hour after listening to the private detective's report, Helen decided to make the phone call. She acknowledged her own nervousness while waiting for the brokerage secretary to connect her.

"Victor Norris."

"Mr. Norris, my name is Helen Riley and I'm interested in opening an account and having you act as my broker. I don't have much to invest yet, but I'd like to meet with you."

\* \* \* \* \*

They dated for three months, were engaged for nine, and married on the anniversary of their first meeting.

"It was love at first sight," Victor told friends and associates.

Helen said the same.

After the wedding, Helen's mother whispered to Helen's father. "She didn't think she would ever get over Mark, but look at her now. Time heals all wounds."

# New Religion

"If you want to get rich," Mondo Mullens said, "start a religion."
He said it so often he finally took himself seriously.

"Mondoism" would combine the most marketable aspects of
several religions—it couldn't fail. The Catholics had costumes, ceremony
and symbolism down to a T. He especially liked the priestly robes and
incense. When properly conditioned, his congregation could be programmed to go into an altered state of consciousness as soon as they
entered the sanctuary and inhaled the nostalgia of patchouli incense.
Baptists were frightened by fire and brimstone preachers, but they sang
upbeat songs, spoke in tongues and had fried chicken dinners. It was
the old fear/fun rollercoaster ride to the pearly gates. New Agers had
channeling, an attention-getter if there ever was one. All you had to do
was close your eyes, distort your features, talk in a weird voice, and
make predictions that couldn't be disproven for five years.

For his religion, Mondo decided to wear an ermine robe and swing
an incense pot while channeling an extraterrestrial. Between profound
messages he would lead the congregation in foot-tapping songs. They
would have bingo on Saturdays and potluck dinners on Sunday afternoons.

All Mondo had to do was fill the rental hall a few times to start the
word-of-mouth referrals that would attract thousands. He fantasized
building his own version of the Crystal Cathedral and establishing a
worldwide television ministry. "Praise be!"

Mondo hired his sister-in-law Amy as marketing director, promising
to pay her when the donations started rolling in. Thirty pounds over-
weight with short brown hair, she strongly resembled a plump Pekingese.

Drawing upon her career background as a Yellow Pages saleswoman, Amy hired a freelance artist to sketch Mondo Mullens dressed in priestly robes and eating fried chicken. The illustration minimized the size of his belly, and a holy aura was airbrushed around his balding head.

Practicing extraterrestrial channeling in front of a mirror, Mondo squinted one eye and spoke out of the corner of his mouth. The facial distortion closed a nostril, which altered his voice. His channeled spirit would speak an octave higher than Mondo and in slow, halting sentences, as if the discarnate was having difficulty using human vocal cords.

Mondo's apartment functioned as the temporary Mondoism operations center. In his spare time he studied tapes of Jane Randini channeling Selka and wondered if Selka was real. Amy watched him scribbling notes as he watched the videos on the living room TV.

"Can ghosts really take over your body and make you talk like that?" she asked.

"Not ghosts, Amy, disembodied spirits. Listen to the wisdom."

Amy watched Jane's pained vocal delivery. It was as if the woman was terribly constipated yet determined to relay a message before the diuretics took effect.

"Are you sure you can do it, Mondo?"

He stopped writing, retrieved the remote from between his legs and pushed the pause button. On the screen, Jane's frozen features expressed great relief or great horror; Amy wasn't sure which.

Mondo shuffled through the stack of books on the coffee table, found the one he was looking for, and handed it to Amy. *How to Verbally Channel Discarnate Spirits.*

"It's just a matter of practice," he said. "Waldorf is anxious to share his wisdom."

"Waldorf?"

"My contact on the other side, a discarnate who exists beyond the veil and wishes to speak through me."

In reality, Mondo had followed the instructions in the book a dozen times, to no avail. No Waldorf. He figured it was best to let Amy think Waldorf was real. Otherwise, when Mondoism became a household word, she might blackmail him or sell the story to a supermarket tabloid.

Amy scanned the contents page of the how-to book. *1. Breathing*

*Exercises; 2. Going Into a Trance; 3. Protection Rituals; 4. Making Contact; 5. Withdrawing to Allow the Spirit to Speak; 6. Awakening.* "What does that mean, 'withdrawing to allow the spirit to speak'?" she asked.

"You have to pull back and let your contact take over. You leave your body and become a distant observer while the entity communicates his wisdom."

"His? Couldn't it be a woman?"

Mondo shrugged. "Waldorf was once a great Pheladian star-fleet commander."

Amy didn't know how to respond to that, so she said, "I've co-ordinated the campaign for next weekend." He was all ears. "For forty dollars the American Legion will rent us a meeting room for 90 minutes Sunday morning."

"How many will it seat?" Mondo wanted to know.

"One hundred."

He seemed pleased. She handed him a copy of the neon pink flyer. "I'm hiring paper boys to insert it in their newspaper deliveries on Friday. Saturday we place the flyer under the windshield wipers of every car in every shopping center in town."

"So be it," he said.

Four thousand flyers were distributed as planned, and preparations were finalized. It was the first step in a campaign lifted right out of the pages of *How to Be a Public Relations Pro* by Jack Williams, the man who helped get presidents elected.

Sunday morning, Mondo and Amy arrived at the rental hall an hour early. The congregation would enter the rectangular shaped room through a back door near the dressing room. The folding chairs were neatly arranged facing the podium on a small stage. "Testing, one, two, three," Mondo said into the microphone. "Am I loud and clear?"

Standing in the back of the room, Amy raised her thumb and smiled.

Mondo gazed upon the empty chairs and contemplated his destiny. Mondoism would fall between Methodist and Mormon in the Yellow Pages. And that was good.

"Better come get dressed, Mondo," Amy called, pulling him out of his reverie.

At 11:00 AM, twenty-seven people were seated in the hall. Mondo had hoped for more, but it would do to start. The law of compounding numbers would do the rest.

Observing through a crack in the dressing room door, Mondo prophesied to Amy, "My congregation will double every week for ten weeks." He whipped an adding machine out of his pocket and ran a quick calculation. "In ten weeks, 13,824 people will attend services."

"Oh, my," she replied, "we'll have to rent the civic auditorium."

Amy snapped a cassette into the boom box. Mondo adjusted the ermine robe he had rented from Cal's Costumes and placed the pointed pope's hat on his head. He lit the incense and blew on it.

Amy opened the door and punched "play" on the cassette deck. Show time!

Elvis Presley sang "Peace in the Valley" as Mondo strutted down the aisle, boom box in one hand, incense pot swinging in the other, smoke trailing behind him like an exhaust. Several people applauded.

At the front of the room, Mondo hung the incense pot on a coat tree and stood behind the podium with his eyes closed while Elvis finished the song. As the last notes faded, Mondo's eyes popped open. He raised his hands pontifically and looked to heaven. "Brothers and sisters, this is the beginning of a new religion for a new age, and you are the founding members of this holy order. Each and every one of you was guided here by your guardian angels to help establish this much-needed ministry."

Next to the podium on a small table sat a bowl of holy water. Mondo dipped his fingers and flicked the liquid in the direction of his audience.

The parishioners—primarily conservatively dressed senior citizens—looked from one to another.

An older man put up his hand, "The flyer said chicken dinners, that right?"

"Right," said Mondo. "from Chunky's Chicken, after the service. Next week, it's potluck."

"When's bingo?" asked a matronly woman.

"Next Saturday night."

Mondo waited to see if there were any other pressing issues, then he said, "We're going to begin with a message from Waldorf, our extraterrestrial contact with the holy order. Although Waldorf exists on a level beyond our understanding, he has the ability to speak directly to you through me."

The audience shifted nervously and watched as Mondo sat on a folding chair beside the podium. "It will take me a few moments to go into trance." He closed his eyes and breathed deeply, just as he'd practiced. He tried to remember the exact words, just in case any of his parishioners had a metaphysical background. "I call out to those on the other side, and to Waldorf in particular. I beseech thee to enter my body as a channel for light and wisdom."

Mondo couldn't remember the protection ritual, so he skipped it and chanted some other things that seemed appropriate. He was distorting his features in preparation for the Waldorf transformation when it happened. One moment he was on top of his act, the next it was as if he'd been slipped a tab of LSD, and a mind movie started to unspool at the edge of perception. He was here, then there—plucked from his body to float in a black void, a disembodied observer of his physical form sitting on a chair beside the podium.

Mondo watched through a misty fog as his body stood up, opened its eyes and bellowed, "WALDORF IS HERE." Arms in the air, he trembled, saying, "I BRING THE WORD . . . THE TRUTH . . . THE FUTURE."

The congregation sat statue still, eyes wide, mouths open.

"BELIEVE IN ME, FOR I OFFER YOU . . . KNOWLEDGE . . . OTHERWISE . . . UNATTAINABLE." Waldorf's voice slowed down, and for a moment he looked like a robot running out of power. One arm froze in the air while his eyes darted about in confusion.

Floating above the congregation, Mondo felt no physical sensations, only the detached sense of an observer watching a play.

"REPENT . . . REPENT . . . REPENT." Like a stuck record. Then Waldorf seemed to power up. His arm came down. "BROTHERS AND SISTERS, DAMNATION IS REALITY. HELL IS A HEARTBEAT AWAY."

All over the room, the parishioners sucked air. A sad-eyed old woman began to cry. Several "Amens" were heard.

"AMEN . . . AMEN . . . AMEN." Waldorf waved his arms. "BUT DO YOU CARE?" Bug-eyed, he leaned forward and visually swept the room, meeting the eyes of the congregation.

Standing by the rear entrance door to usher in any late arrivals, Amy shivered and wished Mondo would come back.

"I DON'T SEE ANY ORANGE," Waldorf shouted.

"What do you mean, *orange*, Brother Waldorf?" asked a fortysomething man in the front row.

"WHAT DO I MEAN? LET HIM WHO HAS EARS TO HEAR, HEAR." Waldorf glared at the questioner. "HOW MANY TIMES HAVE I TOLD YOU TO WEAR ORANGE IN MY HOLY PRESENCE?"

The parishioners looked from one to another and shook their heads. "Never," someone said.

Waldorf looked shocked. "LIES!" he screamed, pounding his fist on the podium. "DO YOU EXPECT TO LIE YOUR WAY TO SALVATION?" With a sweep of his hand the discarnate spirit toppled the podium. It crashed to the floor a few inches from a woman in the front row.

Several people leaped to their feet.

Waldorf stepped into the aisle, waving his arms, spittle drooling from the corner of his mouth.

"DAMNATION TO THE UNBELIEVERS!" He stopped as if remembering something. "PASS THE COLLECTION PLATE, AMY. IT'S TIME THEY SHOWED US THE COLOR OF THEIR MONEY."

"No way, you bully," said a frail-looking woman seated on the aisle. She clutched her purse to her chest.

Floating above the scene in his astral body, Mondo cringed as Waldorf strutted up the aisle to the back of the room where Amy stood by the door.

"OUT OF MY WAY, HARLOT!" She ducked to avoid his trashing arms. "SINNERS!" he roared, twisting the key in the door lock, withdrawing it and putting it in his pocket.

Twenty-seven pairs of eyes, plus Amy's, were glued to Waldorf, who now marched back to the woman clutching her purse and bellowed, "HOW DARE YOU WITHHOLD FROM THIS HOLY MINISTRY?" He snatched the purse from her hands.

"You can't do that in a church of God, Brother Waldorf," said a retirement-aged man in a leisure suit as he followed the preacher back to the podium.

Waldorf, his body shaking with rage, glared at the man for a moment before grabbing the bowl of holy water and dumping it upon the man's head. Enraged, the discarnate bellowed, "WHO ELSE AMONG YOU WISHES TO WITHHOLD YOUR EARTHLY RICHES?"

A scowling, elderly woman stood, turned and began to march toward the door, only to slip in the holy water and collapse to the floor in a howl of pain.

"YOU!" Waldorf pointed at an old man wearing a hearing aid and holding a cane. The man trembled in fear and did not respond. "THE EXPRESSION ON YOUR FACE BETRAYS YOU, SINNER."

Waldorf shook his head and waved his arms. Some of the parishioners were standing. Others were inching their chairs across the floor, subtly trying to distance themselves from Mondo Mullens' new religion. "ONLY I CAN SAVE YOU." Waldorf grabbed a white-haired woman and lifted her in the air. She waved her arms, kicked her feet and sputtered in protest. Waldorf shook her.

"I AM YOUR SALVATION."

From his bird's-eye view, Mondo watched in horror as his parishioners cried and screamed and pounded on the locked door. They were all standing now. Some hysterical, some angry, some advancing toward Waldorf. He watched as a white-haired woman withdrew a long hat pin from her bonnet. A man was swinging the incense pot like a mace, and another man was hefting the coat tree to use as a club.

As quickly as he found himself out of body, Mondo returned in a brief shiver of manifestation. Waldorf was gone and he was instantly aware of his physical senses, the weight of his ermine robe, the sight of the advancing congregation.

"Please, give me a chance to explain," he babbled, backing away. Slipping in the holy water, he fell.

Mondo was attempting to get up as the incense pot whistled into his line of sight and nearly caught him in the forehead. He rolled away, stumbled to his feet and dove for the fire-door exit. Had his congregation been younger they would have caught him, but he cleared the door and shot down the stairs—a priestly butterball in ermine robes descending from on high.

By the time Mondo finished eating Sunday dinner at the Chunky's Chicken on the edge of town, he concluded that he was the victim of religious persecution. Of course, he'd have to move on, like all the religious martyrs that proceeded him. Joan of Arc crossed his mind, but he rejected the gender association. Next time, he decided, he'd go with the Catholic and Baptist touches, but instead of New Age channeling, he'd promote Mormon-style polygamy.

And maybe instead of neon pink flyers, he'd go with purple.

# The Lightbearer

## 1

Lightning slashed the night sky, followed by a roll of rumbling thunder that momentarily drowned the sound of rain hammering the speeding car. Behind the wheel, Jeff LaFayette strained to see the curving mountain road through the deluge assaulting the windshield. The wipers whipped back and forth, leaving only a flash of clarity with each swipe. Hunching forward in the seat, he squinted, clutching the wheel with white-knuckled intensity as he snaked into a curve, side-slipping across the double yellow line. Twisting the wheel in the direction of the skid, he brought the car back into his lane.

He eased off the accelerator.

Dense trees briefly shielded the car from the February storm. The wheels threw up water with the hissing fervor of a pursuing demon. When the windshield began to fog, he snapped the blower switch to high, slid the control bar to defrost.

Fallen branches covered the sign announcing a sharp curve. Jeff accelerated into the turn. He realized his mistake too late, slamming his foot on the brake and clutching the wheel in frozen horror as the car hydroplaned over the rain-slick surface into the guard rail. The railing buckled and snapped, launching the vehicle into an ascending arch out over the treetops, into a timeless space between reality and disbelief — before falling a hundred feet into the storm-swollen creek below.

\* \* \* \* \*

"A damned miracle," the highway patrolman said as he took Jeff's pulse through the shattered window of the crumpled car. "Weak, but alive."

"Think the water saved him?" asked his partner.

"The car must have hit the water flat, then floated the sixty yards down stream to where the creek curves. Water tossed it far enough up on the bank to keep it from sinking."

The second patrolman looked up at the shattered guard rail and visually followed the car's flight path through the broken treetops down to the creek.

\* \* \* \* \*

Jeff awakened in Prescott General Hospital to see Perrin McKinley sitting beside his bed staring at a magazine. She didn't realize he'd opened his eyes, and he stared at her trying to figure out where he was and why his girlfriend was so fuzzy. Even fuzzy, the raven-haired, green-eyed woman was beautiful. Even sitting there in that weird white toga. He shook his head to clear his vision. Mistake.

His moan attracted Perrin. "Jeff? JEFF! Oh, thank God. NURSE!"

The nurse rushed into the room, followed by another. A doctor arrived. Somebody asked Perrin to leave.

"Alahey," Jeff whispered, his voice hoarse and sounding as if it came from far away.

"You can come back in a few minutes," a nurse said, directing Perrin toward the door.

It wasn't a few minutes. It was nearly an hour before a doctor entered the waiting room and asked, "Did Jeff recognize you?" He was a plump, balding man in his early fifties who stood with his shoulders back and his stomach protruding. His manner brusque, businesslike.

"Is he going to be all right, Doctor?"

He nodded, repeated his question.

"Yes," Perrin said. "He seemed to recognize me, but he said something—a word I didn't understand."

"He told me his name is Odin and he lives in Poseidon. When I explained that his name was Jeff LaFayette and he lives in Los Angeles, he seemed momentarily confused, then said, 'Of course.' Does Odin or Poseidon mean anything to you?"

Perrin shook her head. "He doesn't have amnesia?"

The doctor shrugged. "I got him to talk about his life and his career. He said he was en route to Phoenix to play a club date."

"That's true."

The doctor continued, "Then I asked him about the Odin and Poseidon business. He said it must have been a dream or something, because it seemed so real."

Perrin crossed her arms to block a chill coursing through her body. She was dressed warmly in a black Calvin Klein double-breasted blazer, a black turtleneck and black jeans, but the room had turned cold.

Returning to Jeff's room, she found him propped up with a second pillow—his head bandaged, both eyes uniformly blackened. Still connected to an array of blinking electronic monitors, an IV dripped life-sustaining fluid into his unbroken arm.

"You look like a raccoon wearing a turban," she said.

He smiled faintly.

She took his hand, leaned over, kissed his cheek.

"How'd you get here, honey?"

"Your driver's license. An LA cop came knocking on our door. I was afraid you were dead. That was two days ago."

"Two days? I missed the Studio 12 date?"

"Jeff, you won't be working again for months. Anyway, the band met me at the Phoenix airport. They sat with me in the waiting room the first day."

"Where are you staying?" he asked, his voice barely a whisper.

"Local Ramada Inn. There's a bar here called Matt's. The guys picked up a gig backing a local singer. A woman."

"A woman?"

"Those strange creatures with bumpy chests. Some of them sing."

"Jeeze, Alahey."

"Alahey? What's Alahey?"

"You. Alahey. That's your other name in Poseidon."

"You're really scaring me, Jeff."

He looked at her for a long moment, confused, blinking his eyes. "I don't know," he whispered. "It's like I'm two people and I'm drifting back and forth between them. Don't know." He sighed, closing his eyes, his pupils flickering beneath the lids until his breathing deepened.

The monitoring instruments hummed steadily. Perrin assumed he had fallen asleep. She stood looking down at the man she loved, the man she had dated for the last five of her twenty-eight years. They had lived together for eleven months. Home was Venice, California, four doors from the beach and two blocks above the Washington Street pier. It wasn't a safe neighborhood, but it was a vortex of creativity. Their neighbors were artists, writers, actors, and musicians, all living for their day of discovery. Perrin did not number herself among them. She was a computer production artist in a Marina del Rey design studio. Nobody discovered production artists, but they made a better than average living and picked up a check on the first and fifteenth of every month.

Jeff LaFayette and the Bandoleros played the local LA clubs when they could: The Troubadour, The Palomino, China Club. Once in a while they opened for name acts at the Roxy. When their agent couldn't line up local work he sent them on the road.

Perrin walked to the window to see the last remnants of overcast daylight disappearing behind the mountains to the west. Below, the sodium-vapor lamps reflected in parking lot puddles. The weatherman had predicted snow in the higher elevations. Wind-sprayed droplets splattered the window, creating a film of ripples and blurred images.

She wished Jeff hadn't been in an accident. She wished she could see his shoulder-length blond hair now hidden beneath layers of bandages. She wished they were home at the beach. She wished they were married. She wished she could accept her rock and roller for what he was — an irresponsible musician who lived to write songs and sing them to groupies and drunks.

Jeff stirred, whimpered and opened his eyes. Through quivering lips, he slowly formed words. "The law of love is unchangeable . . ."

Perrin watched in worried silence as her lover's eyes drooped, fluttered and closed peacefully. He breathed deeply and his mouth relaxed into a serene smile.

"Good Lord," she said aloud.

\* \* \* \* \*

Jeff was sitting up, busily writing in a notebook when Perrin entered his room the following morning.

"Hi, honey. Have I got a song for you." His voice sounded normal. Beneath the bandages and arm cast, his enthusiasm for life was as evident as ever. The bruises around his eyes had faded to a dull yellow. He thrust the notebook at her.

"Not before I get a kiss," she teased. She took off her wet raincoat and hung it on a hook in the bathroom before accepting the notebook. As she sat in the chair beside the bed, she lovingly took Jeff's hand, noted his excited expression, then looked at the words:

## TRANSCENDENCE
### By Odin

We are the power when we combine
Our thoughts upon a focused line

OHM, NAMMA, CYCLICAL
DRAW DOWN THE LIGHT
OF THE ORACLE

We transcend the body when we align
With the sacred circle beyond time

OHM, NAMMA, ILLUMINATE
THE EXPANDING POWER
OF THE HOLY STATE

Perrin read the words, then read them again. "Jeff, what the hell is going on?"

"Don't you like it?" Disappointment shaded his voice.

She hesitated. "Jeff, you write about broken hearts and resentment of authority. In the five years I've known you, I've never heard you express a spiritual thought much less write spiritual lyrics. And who's this Odin getting the writing credits?"

"I'm Odin. You're Alahey," he said as if there were no question about it.

"Okay," Perrin replied. I need to talk to the doctor, she thought.

"No, you don't need to talk to the doctor, Alahey," Jeff said. "I'm perfectly all right. In fact I feel great."

Perrin looked at him strangely. "How did you know what I was thinking?"

He leaned forward, tapped his index finger on the center of her forehead. "I ran a scan line between my mind and yours. It's as common as talking on Atlantis."

Perrin shivered, didn't respond.

"Honey, everything's great. I spent much of the night accelerating my healing. The concussion is almost handled. It will take a few more days for my broken arm. Look." He shook his head, threw his arms in the air, then snapped them down and pounded on his chest like Tarzan.

Shooting into a standing position, Perrin stumbled backward knocking over the chair. She was about to run out of the room when the doctor walked in.

"Well, I see you've already encountered our medical marvel," he said. "In all my years practicing medicine I've never seen anything like it."

Perrin glanced from the doctor to Jeff and back to the doctor. "He's not the same." she sputtered. "Something weird has happened to him."

"It certainly has," the doctor replied. "If I didn't have the X-rays to prove it, no one would believe it. Literally overnight, Jeff's body has accomplished weeks of healing. It's a true miracle."

Perrin's confusion turned to anger. "For Gods sake, doctor, he thinks he's Odin of Atlantis. That's not a miracle. It's something you should damn well worry about."

"Perrin, I can explain—"

The doctor cut Jeff off in mid-sentence. "Well, I must admit we don't understand that yet, but it hasn't seemed to have reduced his contemporary awareness. Just the opposite in fact."

While the doctor conducted tests on Jeff, Perrin paced the white-walled, white-tiled hospital corridor that smelled of disinfectant. Bored, she took the elevator to the maternity floor and paused at the nursery window where she wistfully watched the ward nurses tending the babies. At this moment the likelihood of marriage and a baby of her own seemed remote.

Jeff spoke the moment Perrin walked back into his room. "We are going to get married and have a baby. I know that, Perrin."

Standing at the foot of his bed, hands clenching the cold metal railing, she said, "Even when I was upstairs, you were reading my mind?

"It's a new ability that's fun to test. I'll stop if you want me to."

"Jeff, I'm going to get you out of this hick-town hospital and home to UCLA Medical Center." Desperation in her voice.

Jeff laughed for the first time since the accident. "I'll be well by tomorrow or the next day."

Perrin sighed loudly, but didn't contradict him.

"Okay, let me try to put it into words you'll understand." Tapping the pen on his notebook, Jeff visually scanned the room before meeting Perrin's emerald eyes. "I'm me, Jeff LaFayette. Okay? I can remember everything that's ever happened to me including the best thing of all, you. I love you just as much now if not more than I did before the accident."

Perrin bit her lip and blinked to withhold tears she felt trembling on her eyelids.

"But," Jeff continued, speaking slowly, feeling his way. "I also have memories of another life that's also mine. You're there but you look different. In the city of Poseidon in the Atlantean lands we went to school together, got married, and had three children. Sometimes when I look at you, Alahey's image and clothing overlay your image." He shrugged his shoulders.

"Are you talking about reincarnation?" Perrin asked. "Memories of a past life?"

"Probably. Back in the seventies I read a book on Edgar Cayce called *The Sleeping Prophet.* I remembered that the Cayce Foundation was in Virginia Beach, so I called this morning and talked to a very helpful lady. From what I described of the Atlantean lifetime that is so familiar to me, she said it was probably after the second catastrophic upheaval, sometime between 28,000 BC and 15,000 BC."

Perrin patted the bed rail in frustration. "This is too much for me," she said, walking back to the chair. "Living one life is difficult enough."

"Perrin, Atlantis is an incredible world. They have electricity, air travel, and natural healing techniques we have yet to discover. They heal with sound, color and vibration."

"TV and jets 28,000 years ago? You're hallucinating."

"No, Perrin. No, I'm not. They don't have television as we know it, but they have mental projection entertainment units that produce the same effect. There are no jets. Atlantean air ships simply reverse gravity. And I think my healing suggests more than hallucination."

She couldn't argue that. "How did you heal yourself?"

"I mentally generated the sound waves and vibrations my body required, while visualizing swimming through a luminous blue healing sea." He took a deep breath and squeezed her hand. "I need you to do something for me."

"What?"

"There must be a metaphysical bookstore or some New Age practitioners in this area. I need a natural quartz crystal, about five to seven inches long. It must be clear with faceted points that aren't chipped."

"All right, I'll see what I can do." A smile forced its way through her mask of uncertainty.

"Can you do it now?" he asked.

"Right now? I just got here."

"It's important. And bring me some clothes." He placed his index finger to the center of his forehead, while touching his thumb to his lips, bowed and closed his eyes.

\* \* \* \* \*

After her first day in Prescott, Perrin decided it was a grey town full of grouchy people, built around a solemn, grey-granite courthouse on a grey plaza square. As she pulled her rented Mustang to the curb in front of a statue memorializing the Rough Riders, she noticed the barred windows on the upper floor of the courthouse. According to an article she'd read in the hospital waiting room, the town was the birthplace of rodeo; a mountain community of retirees, cowboys and transplanted Californians in search of clean air and a better life. From what she'd seen so far, Perrin was sure her fellow Californians had made a terrible mistake.

A metaphysical bookstore sat between a gun shop and a tack store. She searched her purse for parking-meter change, dreading to step out of the car into stabbing rain.

The bookstore clerk said the health food co-op at the other end of town carried crystals.

Wrong. But the co-op manager gave her the name and phone

number of a Reiki therapist who lived in Groom Creek, a community higher up in the mountains. "Shanel has lots of crystals."

"What's Reiki?" Perrin asked the manager, whose hair, wire-rimmed glasses and sack dress labeled her as one of Prescotts' hippie element. There were also "cowboys," "Californians," and "regular people," according to one of the hospital nurses Perrin had talked to over a hospital lunch.

"Reiki is an ancient Tibetan science of energy amplification. It's a way to access and transmit healing."

"People can really do that?" Perrin asked.

The woman nodded. "I'd call Shanel first. You can use the phone on the wall."

Shanel Cleary said she had high quality quartz crystals in the required lengths. "I don't have another Reiki appointment for a couple of hours. I'm only twenty minutes away, so why don't you come on up?" Perrin quickly scrawled the directions on a paper bag.

Turreted Victorians and pitched-roof frame houses lined the street leading out of Prescott into the southern mountains. Three miles up the narrow winding road, scrub growth gave way to pine trees, and the rain turned to splattery slush on the windshield. For the third time in two days Perrin tried to find decent music on the radio. When she finally did it was sandwiched between a commercial for Redman Chewing Tobacco and a community service bulletin announcing lost dogs and cats. She snapped off the radio and wished for a tape player.

At the turnoff, the dirt road became slushy mud. She reduced the car's speed to a crawl. Three or four inches of wet snow covered the ground and clung to low-bending tree branches. Between strands of woods clusters of log and clapboard cabins appeared. Cords of wood were stacked neatly along the walls and beneath decks, ready to fuel fireplaces and wood-burning stoves. White smoke curled lazily from the cabin chimneys before dissipating into the dark, cloud-shrouded sky.

The oversized rural mailbox read "Shanel Cleary." Beneath the name the word REIKI was painted in larger letters. Perrin pulled into the driveway, got out and walked up the steps to the porch of the two-story redwood house. Windchimes hung over the door, cat tracks were imprinted in the snow on the deck railing. She inhaled deeply, appreciating the scent of pine trees and burning fireplaces.

"You must be Perrin. Please come in." Shanel Cleary was fortyish with an oval face, rosy cheeks and friendly smile. Her medium-length brown hair was windblown, and she was dressed in a bulky green sweater, brown-cord pants and men's work boots.

"I've brewed herbal tea. Like some?" Shanel asked as she took Perrin's raincoat and pointed her toward one of the overstuffed chairs forming a half-circle in front of the stone hearth. Fireplace logs hissed and crackled.

"Thank you. I'd love some."

The living room was paneled with rough-sawed redwood planks. Macramé plant holders filled with overflowing greenery hung from the ceiling, the pots twisting slowly in response to the fireplace draft. A lighted display of crystals covered the wall above a Spanish desk. Autumn-hued stained-glass windows cast a warm glow over the room. The picture window framed a distant, snow-capped mountain.

"So you're interested in crystals?" Shanel handed her guest a steaming mug. She sat in the chair next to Perrin. The tea smelled deliciously of orange and cinnamon.

"My boyfriend wants one."

"You don't look like you're from around here," Shanel said.

"Los Angeles."

"I should have guessed," Shanel nodded, smiled. "What is an LA woman doing in Groom Creek, Arizona, looking for crystals?"

Perrin liked her. She explained about Jeff's accident, but didn't mention Atlantis. After several minutes of conversation, she asked, "Do you believe in reincarnation?"

"Of course. I'm too logical not to," Shanel said.

"Logical?"

"Karma and reincarnation is the only belief system that could possibly explain all the injustice and inequality in the world. Organized religions certainly can't."

They had nearly finished their second cup of tea by the time Shanel completed her dissertation on reincarnation. Fascinated, Perrin decided to confide Jeff's experiences to her.

"Just like Peter Hurkos," Shanel said.

Perrin looked at her blankly, not recognizing the reference.

"In the 1940s Peter Hurkos fell thirty feet from a ladder and fractured his skull. While recovering in the hospital, he discovered he was clairvoyant; he knew things about his fellow patients. Later he worked with the police to help solve over fifty murders, including the Boston Strangler case."

"But Jeff isn't psychic. He thinks he's two people."

"No, he's just remembering a past life, Perrin. And he's drawing upon ancient awareness to heal himself in the present." Shanel settled back into the chair and propped her feet on the hearth. "He wants the crystal as a power source."

"Do you think he can use it to further accelerate the healing?" Perrin asked.

"Very likely." Shanel rubbed her temples. "All your past-life memories are recorded in the memory banks of your subconscious mind. Usually they can only be accessed through hypnotic regression or in dreams. But Jeff's accident somehow released his awareness."

Perrin nodded, still confused.

"And you're there, too. You might be soulmates. I'll bet when you met Jeff it was an electric experience."

"For both of us. We took one look at each other, and we both knew what was going to happen." Perrin smiled at the warm memory.

"I hope he doesn't have any of the dangerous knowledge," Shanel said. "Many believe it was the amplified power of crystals that destroyed the Atlantean civilization."

* * * * *

On the way back to the hospital, Perrin turned into the McDonald's® drive-through window in Prescott. She nibbled Chicken McNuggets® and sipped a Diet Coke® while driving the rain-swept streets back to the hospital. Lightning ripped open the sky behind the mountains, followed by ominous peals of thunder that sent shivers down her spine. The windshield wipers flicked hypnotically at the throbbing rain. The car's heater wheezed out stale rubbery-smelling air. Great junk-food dinner environment, she thought. But better than eating alone in the plastic-coated Golden Arches.

Jeff was sitting in a hallway chair when Perrin stepped out of the hospital elevator. He grinned like he'd won the lottery, his eyes flashing excitement.

"Jeff, for heaven's sake, what are you doing out of bed?"

He stood and extended his arms. They kissed passionately for so long a white-haired man in a wheelchair applauded their display. Perrin smiled, blushed.

"I want you," Jeff whispered softly in her ear.

She buried her head in his shoulder with a muffled, "Three days ago you were nearly dead."

"This Atlantis stuff is hot," he said. He drew her arm through his for the walk back to his room. "There's a nurse on the afternoon shift that I recognized from back there."

"Back where?"

"Atlantis. I see an image of her Atlantean body superimposed over her current body. It's like watching a movie projected over the person. She was one of the Children of the Law of One."

"Did you tell her she was 28,000 years old?"

"Did you get me a crystal?"

Perrin opened her purse, took out a velvet-wrapped object. Their eyes met in a flicker of anticipation, as he unwrapped the prize and gasped in disbelief.

"Oh, baby, this is better than . . ." The words caught in his throat as he lifted the silver wand. A perfect seven-inch quartz crystal projected from the end.

"A Hopi silversmith made the wand. It's your birthday present and next year's Christmas present combined." A glint of humor in her voice.

Jeff held the wand in his right hand, closed his eyes, opened them, closed them again and breathed deeply. For an instant she thought the wand had begun to glow. *Impossible!*

"Incredible!" he said. "Just incredible!"

"I bought myself some crystal earrings. Like them?" From each ear two-inch quartz crystals dangled from silver Hopi conchos. Jeff nodded his approval and returned his attention to the wand. Perrin said, "I talked to someone who helped me understand, but I'm still having a hard time putting all this together. What are you going to do with the crystal?"

"I'd rather wait and show you," he said. "Let's just watch TV and relax for a while." He pressed a button on the remote control and the wall-mounted set flickered to life. He flipped through the channels to MTV — thundering guitar riffs amid quick cuts of young men on a smoky stage.

Perrin scooted her chair closer to the bed so she could lay her head on the mattress and hold Jeff's hand. After watching nearly an hour of music videos, the female VJ announced an environmental news report. An animated chart explained the benefits of recycling aluminum cans. Perrin closed her eyes and was nearly asleep when she was pulled back into reality by Jeff squeezing her hand tighter and tighter. It was beginning to hurt. She jerked free, but he didn't seem to notice.

"Kesar reborn," Jeff growled. "God help us."

Perrin looked at him. "Jeff, snap out of it. I'm getting real sick of this weirdness."

"God help us," he said again. The silver rod was clenched in his right hand, the crystal pulsing blue and intensifying in color.

Perrin stared in disbelief. Slowly she stood up and inched away from the bed. Jeff was scrutinizing the man on TV. *"This afternoon Senator Charles Ames spoke to the Concerned Citizens' Committee about his plans to build a solar-laser power generator in the San Joaquin Valley."* The camera panned a crowd of people carrying American flags, then cut to a medium close-up of a ruggedly handsome white-haired man in his mid-fifties who punctuated his words with vehement gestures. "The generator will provide clean power and set a new standard of environmental safety."

"No-o-o-o-o." The word skirled balefully out of Jeff's mouth. He raised the silver rod and the air crackled with electricity as the crystal pulsed luminescent blue. An audible hum seemed to emanate from everywhere, growing louder until it became a shrill whine that made Perrin's head hurt.

She covered her ears, backing up until she felt the icy window against her back. Outside, a flash of lightning eerily projected her shadow and the rivulets of rain onto the walls. She shivered uncontrollably.

"No-o-o-o-o," Jeff growled again, pointing the rod at the TV screen. A jagged phosphorescent blue blast shot out of the crystal with a crackling hiss. The TV screen exploded, slivers of shattered glass and plastic showering the room and ricocheting against the window. Smoking fragments landed in Perrin's hair and on her clothing, their heat scorching her skin. She shook herself violently, clawing at her hair as she stumbled away from the window and into the corner where she huddled against the walls.

The air stank of ozone and burned plastic. A smoky cloud floated over the scene like a malevolent apparition attempting to take physical form.

A nurse burst into the room. "What happened?" she shouted. "Are you all right?"

## 2

"Sounds like Jeff's crossed over into the Twilight Zone," said Patrick Lee, the Bandoleros' bass player and harmony singer. He stood by the motel room window looking out at the highway. The rain had finally turned to wind-driven snow that encrusted one side of the trees and road signs, swirling crazily through the eerie illumination of the parking lot lights. At 2 AM, only an occasional vehicle inched along the unplowed highway into Prescott.

Perrin sat on one of the double beds while drummer Danny Torres stretched out on the other bed. Keyboard player Townsend DeCamma sat cross-legged on a chair.

"What did he say about the fried TV set?" Townsend asked.

"I think he was as shocked as I was," Perrin replied. "I ran out. I couldn't deal with it."

Danny waved a bottle at Perrin and asked if she wanted a shot of Jack Daniels®. She shook her head. She wanted to tell the band how much she loved Jeff and how scared she was, but there was no point. Road-weary LA musicians were a unique breed of detached cynics.

Everyone jumped at the intense knock on the door. "Go away," Danny shouted.

"Probably a groupie who followed you home from the bar," Perrin laughed.

Townsend answered the door. "Jeff! How the hell did you get out of —"

Jeff brushed past him into the room. There was no cast on his arm. His head bandages had been removed and although his blond hair was matted, he looked normal.

"Jeff, what are you doing?" Perrin was standing, her hands to her mouth.

He kissed her on the cheek. "The crystal."

They were still talking when dawn sliced across the eastern horizon to cast a rosy glow over the snowbound world. Jeff had answered their questions for three hours. He had focused his newfound knowledge of Atlantean healing techniques through the crystal, accelerating his healing. Sneaking out of the hospital was easy. Finding help to take off the cast was harder, but he'd done it.

"You can't skip out on the bill," Perrin said.

"They have my insurance information. Had I stayed, they would have stalled my release and ten doctors would have given me the third degree. Better this way."

"Why did the senator upset you so much?" Townsend said.

"There are two sociopolitical factions on Atlantis. The Children of the Law of One are spiritual and concerned with the greater good. The Sons of Belial crave material pleasures and power. Senator Charles Ames is an Atlantean leader named Kesar, a Son of Belial responsible for thousands of deaths."

"But even if this reincarnation stuff is for real, Jeff, that was then and this is now."

"I could sense his evil. He hasn't changed. His project has the potential to harm millions."

The band members glanced at each other, then returned their attention to Jeff. No one was willing to challenge him.

"What the hell did you do on Atlantis?" Patrick asked. "Did everyone have the ability to heal themselves and zap things with crystal rods?"

"Third-caste priests are trained from birth to do these things."

"Let's see ya blow up the TV with your rod," Danny snickered. The Jack Daniels® was catching up with him.

"No way," Perrin snapped. "We're going to my room and to bed." She stood and took Jeff's arm. He followed obediently.

Despite their lack of sleep, they showered together, soaping each other sensually. Jeff was first into bed, pulling Perrin down on top of him. "This isn't fair," she whispered. "All you have to do is tap into your crystal for a recharge."

"I'd rather tap into you for a recharge."

Later, Perrin settled cozily into the familiar crook of her lover's arm. "At least you still make love like the old Jeff," she whispered.

The last thing she remembered before falling asleep was Jeff saying, "The band can do their gig with the lady singer. I have to stop Kesar."

\* \* \* \* \*

The flight from Phoenix Sky Harbor to LAX took an hour. Perrin's Ford Probe GT was parked on the top floor of the short-term lot. A film of dehydrated smog and jet fuel covered the vehicle. Slipping behind the wheel, she snapped the unlock button and Jeff swung into the passenger seat. It took her longer to find the parking receipt than it did to exit the airport and reach Lincoln Boulevard. Ten minutes later she pulled into the parking slot behind their Venice apartment.

"God, it feels good to be home," Jeff shouted, leaping out of the car. He ran the seventy-five yards down the alley to the beach.

Perrin hurried to catch him.

"In Atlantis we live on a cliff above the sea," he said, putting his arm around her waist.

"Lived, Jeff," Perrin corrected. "Past tense. We're not there anymore."

"Maybe none of this is an accident," he said, looking up at the cloudless sky. The light breeze rustled the palm trees lining the beach sidewalk. In-line skaters and bicyclists jockeyed for position along the walkway.

Hand-in-hand, Jeff and Perrin walked out on the sand, skirting a volleyball game and avoiding a panhandler. At the water's edge they took off their shoes, rolled up their pants, waded into the surf.

"Maybe it's all happening for a purpose." He looked deeply into the eyes of the woman he loved. "Maybe it's my karma."

"Maybe we should just be grateful you're still alive, and we have each other, and we live where we live," Perrin said.

Her loving smile touched his heart.

\* \* \* \* \*

Perrin arrived home from work Monday evening to find Jeff sitting on the floor in the middle of the living room, surrounded by photocopies of newspaper stories, magazine articles and environmental reports.

"All on Senator Ames, I assume?" She tossed her purse into a chair, and carefully stepped across the papers to kneel and kiss Jeff.

"I'm beginning to see what he's up to." He waved a piece of paper.

"Tell me at dinner." She began stripping off clothing as she headed toward the bedroom.

Five minutes later Perrin emerged in pink cotton sweats. Jeff didn't look up as she walked through the room. She envied his ability to focus on the project at hand.

The apartment was furnished in southwestern decor, with Taos and Mexican furniture. Special touches included Tabasco-mahogany half-paneling and an iron-spotted gold-brick fireplace. Photos, paintings and Indian weavings were clustered in design groups on the walls.

The aroma of cumin-spiced beans soon permeated the apartment. Dinner was a Perrin McKinley special: fruit salad, vegetarian chili and cornbread. They ate on a table inlaid with Mexican tiles. Perrin lit candles. A stained-glass lamp cast a soft glow in the corner.

"Senator Ames is using environmental interest to generate support." He held a piece of cornbread in one hand, drumming the fingers of his other hand on the table. "They won't discover the full potential until the project is complete. In addition to nuclear reactors and atom bombs, we'll have laser amplification to deal with. It's just as deadly and could be developed by unstable third world nations."

"You can't know that for sure," Perrin said.

"I know it for sure. On Atlantis, Kesar was the man behind a solar-laser generation project meant to triple the power output of the Locoren Plains. Our best scientists warned that a power block could create a surge that would set off a chain reaction. Kesar ignored the advice and overrode the recommendations by discrediting some fine men."

"What happened?"

"A catastrophe. A surge started fires in every structure on the plains. Imagine a city of half a million people in flames. Over a hundred thousand died." Jeff looked away from the dinner table into the living room and the stacks of papers he'd arranged on the floor. "Of course, Kesar placed the blame on others and walked away to create new projects for his own benefit."

"What did I do on Atlantis, Jeff? I'm not saying I accept all this, but..."

"You're an artisan, a sculptor. You show your work in spiritual shrines. We are considered a vibrationally compatible couple—that means we harmonize. We have two sons and a daughter."

"I'm afraid I just can't picture you as a priest."

"Church and state are one and the same, but the religion contains no fear. Priests are more like the congressmen of today, only there are a lot more of us."

Bemused, Perrin shook her head slowly. "At lunch I bought some books." She held up a paperback and opened the book to a marked page. "Let me read you something and you tell me if it's accurate, okay?"

Jeff tilted back in his chair.

*"Atlantean society in its most evolved form allowed freedom of expression and purpose, and encouraged those belonging to the upper castes to become all they were capable of being. The island continent was populated by people of different races and colors, but the majority of Atlanteans had black hair and a skin color like that of the American Indians. Women were considered equal to men, but during periods when they outnumbered men, polygamy was encouraged and men could lawfully marry two wives."*

Perrin looked at Jeff and scowled playfully.

*"Marriage was based on vibrational compatibility, and the ceremony was performed by a temple priest or priestess. If the relationship didn't work, the union was dissolved by the temple authorities without any unpleasantness. Those who did not want to marry were encouraged to have lovers and out-of-wedlock children, if both parents were good mental and physical specimens. A large number of women worked as surrogate mothers in state-run child-rearing centers.*

*"Many young people were drafted to serve the greater good of the society in a capacity best suited to their talents. This often meant being assigned to a specific technical school, which left the individual no choice as to his life's work.*

*"The country was ruled by an emperor and divided into provinces managed by appointed viceroys. The viceroys were responsible for governing their own province and for ensuring the well-being of the people. This included overseeing agricultural development. Harvested crops were distributed equally among the people of the province."*

Perrin hesitated. "Sounds a bit too socialistic for me."

"Please, continue," Jeff said.

"At the bottom of the Atlantean caste system were the mutants or 'things.' These were lifeform experiments that had failed, trapping entities in hideous bodies – some half-man, half-animal, others human but with gruesome appendages. The mutants labored as slaves, often on farms. Next came the common laborers, production workers, and servants. Technical workers, artisans, and researchers stood one rung higher, and next to the top of the system were seven levels of elders and priests. The top of the system was comprised of the viceroys and the emperor. The color of the belt each priest wore around their waist indicated their level of awareness.

"Upper-class women wore tunics or gowns, of various lengths. Men dressed in tunics, kilts, and sandals. Clothing was usually white or a very light pastel.

"Psychic abilities were highly respected and encouraged, especially among the upper classes. Those who were naturally empathic and developed their gifts ranked high in the caste system. Psychic development was taught in the schools, and there was a time when everyone was connected psychically. When the mind-link was misused for selfish purposes, the people were forced to disconnect en masse.

"Crystals played an important part in Atlantean life and were used primarily to heal and to project the power of the mind. The Atlanteans beamed light through crystals, transmitting different healing rays to regenerate tissue and organs. Vibrational sound chambers were also used as part of the physical and/or mental healing process. At the age of ten, children began to study the subtleties of vibrational sound in school.

"The Atlanteans believed in an all-powerful Supreme Being, symbolized by the sun or a circle. They considered their god so omnipotent that his name could not be mentioned, except as an O sound that was hummed as 'aum'."

Perrin stopped reading and put down the book. "Atlantis certainly doesn't sound like any great society to me. Prejudicial caste systems? People assigned to their life's work? Is this accurate, Jeff?"

He nodded. "Generally, yes. The mutant things were long before my time. I've never heard of men marrying two women. If accurate, maybe that's something that happened later. But the system worked better than any in known history. Atlantis enjoyed thousands of years of peace and prosperity. Of course, in Odin's time there was . . . is growing dissension between the Children of the Law of One and Sons of Belial."

"I wish you'd forget about this Senator Ames business," Perrin said, beginning to clear the table.

"I'll be gone for the next couple of days," Jeff replied. "I need to do some research."

## 3

The flyer was printed in black ink on bright green paper.

### A DEMONSTRATION
### OF ATLANTEAN POWER
### WILL TAKE PLACE
### AT 8 PM, FRIDAY, FEBRUARY 22.

*At this time, I will blow up the capstone of the Beverly Hills City Hall with the power of my mind projected through an ordinary quartz crystal.*

*The reason for this demonstration is to direct public attention to an important environmental message I will deliver in front of the Federal Building on Wilshire Boulevard at noon the next day.*

"For God's sake, Jeff, you disappear for two whole days and the moment I step in the door you hand me this? Are you crazy?" Perrin put down the flyer and looked directly into his excited eyes.

"Honey, I have to do something. This will make the public listen."

"This will get you put in jail, Jeff." she countered. "What is it you have to say that the public needs to hear?" She took off her sportcoat and dropped wearily into a living room chair. Jeff sat in a chair across from her.

"Everything is happening awfully fast," he said. "But our country is racing headlong into environmental devastation. Senator Ames is doing all he can to speed it along. If I'm dramatic enough, the media will cover it. I'll blow the capstone at eight to assure we get coverage on the eleven o'clock news. People will have to listen on Saturday."

Perrin shook her head. "Jeff, damn it! Slow down. If you were a priest on Atlantis, why did you reincarnate as a rock n' roller who can't get a record deal or sell a song? It's not logical. I know you want publicity, but this isn't the way to get it."

"Perrin, Atlantis made some of the same mistakes we're making today and they paid a terrible price. I'm not seeking publicity for myself."

"Aren't you? You've never been concerned about the environment before. Hell, you throw beer cans out the car window."

"If you won't help me, I'll do it myself," he snapped.

"Help you? Do you really think I'll help you blow up City Hall?" Exasperation in her voice. "Jeff, I think you need help."

"Yeah," he said, standing up. "I need your help, and obviously I'm not going to get it."

Perrin heard the kitchen door slam. Moments later, a car motor was gunned twice before rumbling down the alley.

\* \* \* \* \*

Jeff purchased more green paper in a stationery store and ran off the flyers for the Friday demonstration on a do-it-yourself copy machine in Westwood. They were mailed to all Los Angeles newspapers, radio and television stations, environmental organizations, and every city official Jeff could find listed. He also dispensed copies around the nearby UCLA campus. The 1,000 flyers he would pass out on Saturday he had printed in green ink on white paper. Because they were less subversive he gave the job to a quick print shop in Santa Monica. Santa Monica was used to radical activists.

Sitting in a rented Chevy Beretta parked in the Beverly Hills Library parking lot, across the street from City Hall, Jeff fingered the silver rod, rolling it over and over in his hand. He'd spent hours practicing on a deserted cove above Ventura. If he went into a self-imposed, altered state of consciousness to enhance his psychic energy, it greatly increased the amount of power he could focus through the crystal. The cliffs of the cove were now pocked with circular holes that no one but a few sunbathers would notice.

Though he tried to focus on the plan, his thoughts kept wandering to Perrin. He couldn't blame her for not wanting any part of this. She couldn't understand his obsessive need to act—a need fueled by terrible memories of another time and another place.

If the media thought there was any chance he would make an attempt on the capstone, they'd be sure to cover the story. He guessed a few of the stations would gamble one reporter and a cameraman. The police would be there for sure. So would a lot of UCLA students with nothing better to do than check it out.

Jeff pulled slowly out into the Thursday afternoon traffic. BMWs, Mercedes and Jaguars shot past him, carrying the rich and famous to their dates with destiny. Jeff had to practice some more before he was ready to meet his fate in the badlands of Beverly Hills.

* * * * *

Perrin left work early on Friday. From her apartment she called everyone who might know of Jeff's whereabouts. No one had heard from him. She watched the local news. There was no mention of any threat to Beverly Hills city property. By 6 PM her anxiety had escalated into a frenzied fear that corkscrewed through her stomach, stealing her breath.

The sky was dark by 6:20 as she drove east on Wilshire Boulevard. Light rain misted the windshield by the time she reached Beverly Hills. As the lighted Civic Center loomed into view she noted the ongoing City Hall restoration project. Architects had combined Art deco with southwestern step designs of green, red and pink ceramic tile. As an artist, Perrin thought they mixed like oil and water. "Only in California," said the critics. Only in Beverly Hills, thought Perrin.

Until the restoration project was completed, the Beverly Hills Police Department was located in temporary wooden structures running the full block in front of City Hall. The sight sent goosebumps running up and down her arms. He wouldn't. He couldn't, she thought. Not under the circumstances. But knowing Jeff, she was sure he would.

Barricades blocked Crescent Drive and a uniformed policeman turned all traffic left, away from City Hall, back into the business section of the city. She turned right on Rodeo Drive and then east to find a metered parking place on the far side of the park that lined Santa Monica Boulevard. Hundreds of young people were milling around in the park.

UCLA kids, she thought. They're here to watch Jeff blow up the capstone. Oh, God!

Perrin shielded her eyes from the misting rain. A block away, the golden-arched turret sat on top of a colorful mosaic dome capping the nine-story City Hall. Spotlighted against the black sky, it glistened for everyone to see. Challenging Jeff to send it into another dimension.

At the edge of the grass, a homeless man with a bedroll leaned against a sign: "The Use Of This Park Is Prohibited Between the Hours of 11:00 PM and 6:00 AM." Perrin walked through the chattering, trendily dressed young men and women to the center of the park and the Hunter and Hounds statue—an appropriate metaphor, she thought. It was 7:05 PM.

Turning slowly, she wondered where Jeff would be. She wanted to talk him out of it. She wanted to take him home and make love to him. She wanted him to forget about Atlantis.

The park ran two blocks long and a half block wide, the turreted capstone visible from anywhere on the green and from blocks in other directions. Jeff was a needle in a haystack. She started her search at the east end of the park, crisscrossing back and forth through throngs of people casting dubious glances at the capstone. "Two to one, nothing happens," said a blond-haired kid with a crew cut.

"It will be a religious sign," said a conservative-looking girl.

"It would take a bazooka," said someone else.

"Just one of those green-earth radicals," said another.

After walking the first block, Perrin recognized the futility of her efforts. She might have passed him. A breeze now whipped the spitty February rain, soaking her cotton jacket. Hunching, she jammed her hands deeper into her pockets to fight the chill. At the public restrooms and phone center she ducked under the alcove to get out of the rain. Her makeup was surely running, but she didn't care.

It was 7:40 when she finished crisscrossing the second block of the park; 7:50 by the time she had checked the library parking lot and grounds. As she made her way back across Santa Monica Boulevard to the park, she noticed numerous policemen infiltrating the crowd. On the sidewalk, a TV cameraman was locking his camera to a tripod, its lens trained on the capstone. An assistant held an umbrella to shield the camera from the rain.

"Hi," Jeff said, taking her by the arm.

"JEFF! I've been looking—"

"I'm parked over there, come on."

They walked down the sidewalk, past the TV camera, across the street and into an alley between the multimillion dollar homes on the far side of the park. Jeff unlocked the door of the Beretta; Perrin slipped into the passenger seat. He circled behind the car to the driver's door and withdrew the glowing crystal rod from his coat pocket. Raising the rod to his line of sight, he aimed at the capstone nearly a block away. A shimmering, iridescent beam of blue light crackled and hissed from the tip of the crystal. The golden turret exploded without a sound. Glittering metallic pieces showered down upon the roofs and courtyard of the unfinished Civic Center. A roar went up from the crowd in the park. Jeff lowered the rod, nodding in satisfaction. Moving briskly, he opened the car door and eased behind the wheel. The motor rumbled to life, and he drove quietly down the alley into the splendor of the Beverly Hills neighborhood.

* * * * *

A slow-motion shot of the capstone exploding ran four times on KABC between 8:30 and 11:00 PM as a news teaser, and was the lead story on the eleven o'clock news. The feature began with a close-up of Jeff's flyer, followed by coverage of the UCLA students in the park. The explosion was shown in real time and in slow motion. The next shot was of the alley. "Witnesses say the beam emanated from this alley. On either side are the homes of the rich and famous." The camera panned the neighborhood. "Although no one saw a car it is assumed that one was used. As you can see the police are making tire and footprint castings."

Perrin and Jeff watched the news in bed, limbs sensually tangled under sheets still sweaty from making love.

"It really happened, didn't it?" Perrin's voice was a whisper of disbelief.

The camera cut to a medium close-up, split-screen shot of two men. The male news anchor on the left said, "This is Doctor Alan Shelton, a renowned physicist and NASA research scientist who has agreed to talk to us via satellite. Doctor, how could someone have destroyed the City Hall capstone with a beam of blue light?"

Doctor Shelton, a thin, solemn man in his sixties, appeared camera shy. "Well, apparently it was accomplished with laser technology.

105

In theory such a thing is possible with a relatively small weapon, but we don't know of any such working model."

"Then you don't accept that someone could have destroyed the capstone by projecting the power of his mind through a quartz crystal, as the perpetrator claimed in the flyer?"

"Such powers exist only in science fiction."

"But if the government has no knowledge of this power, does it mean that a terrible new weapon is now in the hands of radical activists?"

"I'm not qualified to respond to that question."

"Okay. Doctor, what can you tell us about military applications of laser technology?"

"Lasers harness atoms to store and emit light in a coherent fashion. The electrons in the atoms of a laser medium are energized to an excited state by an energy source, then stimulated to emit the stored energy as a beam. In theory, lasers could destroy hostile ballistic missiles, as in the Star Wars defense system President Ronald Reagan wanted to build. Guidance systems for missiles, aircraft, and satellites are in various stages of development. Senator Charles Ames is sponsoring a bill to build the first solar-laser amplification generator as an alternative to nuclear—"

The anchorman interrupted. "But you're sure that the energy of a human mind couldn't excite the electrons and focus the energy emission?"

"The human mind could never do such a thing. I'd stake my reputation on it."

The camera cut back to the female anchor in the studio. "According to the flyer that announced tonight's demonstration, the person or group responsible will deliver their environmental message in front of the Federal Building in Westwood at noon tomorrow. I'm sure federal agents and a few policemen will be there too. Channel Seven News will also be there to cover the story."

Jeff propped his head on his arm. "During the two days I was away, I read the *Edgar Cayce On Atlantis* book you bought. Back in the thirties Cayce described the power of light projected through crystals. He predicted this Atlantean power source would be rediscovered in the United States in 1958. Two American physicists filed a laser patent application in 1958."

"You heard what the newscaster said, Jeff. Federal agents, cops. We're talking jail time."

"Wire services, networks and major news magazines will also be there," Jeff said. "We're talking an unparalleled communications opportunity."

One of the flyers Jeff planned to distribute at the Federal Building lay on the bedside stand. Perrin picked it up to read again. She had been nearly hysterical during the drive home from Beverly Hills, but Jeff had talked to her calmly, explaining and re-explaining. By the time they made love, the dread was receding, but she knew the fears were only swept into the dark corners of her mind; they weren't gone. When the glow of tranquillity faded they would crawl, growling and snarling, back out into the light of reality.

The second flyer read:

GET INVOLVED!
STOP SENATOR CHARLES AMES'
SOLAR-LASER POWER AMPLIFICATION PROJECT
*BEFORE IT DESTROYS US!*
LASER ENERGY GENERATORS
WILL EVENTUALLY DESTROY OUR CIVILIZATION
UNLESS WE DISMANTLE THE EXISTING FACILITIES
AND STOP FURTHER DEVELOPMENT OF
SOLAR-LASER POWER AMPLIFICATION

My name is Jeff LaFayette. After nearly dying in an automobile accident last week in Prescott, Arizona, I awakened with complete memories of an Atlantean lifetime and with the developed abilities of that incarnation. One example is the projection of my will through a quartz crystal as demonstrated in Beverly Hills last night. The doctors in Prescott will verify that my body, in two days, accomplished weeks of healing. I do not expect you to believe my words initially, but you cannot deny my abilities.

I stand before you today for one reason only: to point out that the Ames solar-laser generator is as dangerous as a nuclear reactor, and in many ways more dangerous because it can be easily converted to offensive weaponry and duplicated. I am speaking from my Atlantean experience. The project must be stopped, and I call upon peace advocates and environmentalists everywhere to assist me in accomplishing this goal.

Thank you for listening.


"Is it coincidence, Jeff? Ames building a laser-powered generator and you awakening with your Atlantean abilities?"

"My Atlantean parents died in the fires that swept the Locoren Plains," Jeff said softly.

Perrin folded the flyer into a paper airplane, flicked it into the air, watched it shoot across the room toward the dresser, dip, circle and return to land on her stomach. "How can I help you tomorrow?" she asked.

## 4

Jeff spent Saturday morning in meditation while Perrin kept busy cleaning the apartment. When she was a teenager, her mother assigned her Saturday chores to keep her from working herself into a dither over a date that evening. It seemed a lifetime ago, Woodland Hills in the seventies. She remembered her father teasing her about her dithers. He'd say, "A dither is a state of vacillation or flustered excitement or fear. You're dithered, dear."

"It's appropriate for today," she said out loud as she scoured the bathroom wash basin.

"What's appropriate?" Jeff asked from the doorway.

"Dither. I'm in a dither. Want to make something of it, buddy?" She laughed.

Jeff shook his head. "It's almost time to go."

The bumper-to-bumper Saturday morning traffic on Wilshire became gridlocked as they neared the 405 overpass.

"All these people couldn't be going to the Federal Building, could they?" Perrin said.

At the Wilshire overpass, the police diverted inbound traffic onto the southbound 405. "Maybe they'll let us through if I explain I'm the star attraction," Jeff said, glancing at Perrin. She huddled in the passenger seat, her left hand clutching her throat.

"Maybe you could just hand them a flyer as you run the barricade," she replied.

Jeff followed the traffic up the ramp and onto the freeway, exiting at the first off-ramp, then winding through back streets to within two blocks of the Federal Building. They parked on a neighborhood street of 1940s bungalows with fully-grown palm trees standing sentry in curbside rows.

"These used to be working-class homes," Jeff said as he got out of the car. "Today they cost a quarter million or more. I don't know how any fixed-income or working-class stiff could afford one."

The rain had stopped during the night. The day was grey, blustery, and threatening. Perrin wore her dangling crystal earrings, a blue Ford racing jacket, faded 501 jeans and boots. Jeff wore a wool herringbone sport coat, a black shirt, black jeans, and basketball shoes. He took a box of flyers from the trunk and handed Perrin the Beretta car keys. Then arm in arm they walked down the sidewalk, past a young boy on his bicycle, an old woman unloading sacks of groceries from her car, and a pot-bellied man cutting grass with a sputtering power mower.

At 11:45 they reached the Federal Building, which sat in the middle of a square block of well-kept lawn. Located in Westwood, the building often served as the site of activist demonstrations. Today, thousands of people spilled over into the blockaded city streets. Policemen were everywhere.

"Oh-h-h-h-h, Jeff. Please, let's rethink this," Perrin said as they began to squeeze their way through the excited crowd.

Jeff thrust a stack of flyers into her hand. "Give them out," he yelled over the din. Someone whipped a large Greenpeace flag back and forth over the heads of the crowd. The ground was littered with "Earth First" flyers. As they made their way slowly toward the center of the lawn, they passed people carrying posters, some handprinted, others professionally done: *Support Women's Rights. Ban Animal Testing. Down With Proposition 109. Save Santa Monica Bay.*

Men were silhouetted against the sky on the roof of the 17-story building. Probably a SWAT team, Jeff thought. A crane lifted a television cameraman high above the throng. Overhead, a helicopter maintained its position above the building, twirling lazily in the sky like some huge insect, the downdraft throwing up swirling debris.

Shielding his eyes, Jeff searched for the ideal position and decided it would be in the crane bucket with the cameraman. It was 12:01 by the time they maneuvered beneath the crane. Jeff stopped, closed his eyes for a moment, took a deep breath and drew the glowing, pulsating crystal rod from his right-hand pocket. Pointing it at the crowd in front of him, he began to release the energy, pushing them back. At first the people didn't realize what was happening. Then some began screaming in fear, others in excitement. Jeff, with Perrin at his side, began to turn slowly, pushing the people back. They completed the turn and he intensified the energy, turning again and again until a twenty-foot circular force field was in place.

A uniformed policeman shoved his way through the crowd and slammed into the force field. His face flushed with anger as he drew his service automatic and ordered Jeff and Perrin to surrender. Moments later, a plainclothesman made his way to the cop, showed him a badge and ordered the man to put away his gun.

Perrin motioned for the TV cameraman to lower the crane. She watched him communicate with someone over his headset, before the crane bucket began to slowly descend. Jeff lowered the crystal, its blue light throbbing like a heartbeat. When the bucket reached ground level Jeff said, "Could we come up with you?"

The cameraman was a paunchy, middle-aged man whose round face wore a cautious grin. "Be my guest," he said, "But there's only room in here for one of you." He offered Jeff a hand.

"Be right back," Jeff said to Perrin, kissing her quickly. A moment later the bucket ascended into the air. Jeff now held the crystal skyward, the blue beam hissing and crackling lightning-like blasts into the dark clouds that hung over the scene like a shroud. With his left hand he threw the flyers into the wind. They floated out over the milling thousands to be snatched from the air by the curious, activists, media, and police alike.

The cameraman tapped Jeff on the shoulder. "We're live. The camera on the truck over there is covering us. Do you want to say anything?" The man was taking off his headset as he spoke.

"Yes, I do," Jeff said. As he spoke he noticed a man in a top-coat grasping Perrin's arm, pulling her away. "Leave her alone!" Jeff screamed. When the man didn't release her, Jeff raised the rod and unleashed his anger through the crystal. A pulsating burst of blue light snapped and sizzled off the tip. The target shot backward into the crowd as if kicked by a horse, then doubled forward, screaming in agony as he pitched face first to the ground.

Perrin fell in the other direction, leaped to her feet and bolted into the crowd, whose attention was still focused on Jeff. Pushing deeper into the layers of humanity, she could still see policemen clearing the field beneath the crane bucket. She worked her way deeper into the crowd and turned just in time to see the crane bucket topple out of the sky, hitting the ground with an earthshaking thud.

"JEFF!" she screamed, unable to see what was happening on the ground twenty feet in front of her. The crowd panicked and began moving mindlessly, some shoving forward, others trying to move away. She struggled to breathe in the crush of people. Screaming sirens sliced through the mass hysteria like banshees warning of horrors to come. The helicopter descended until the thumping roar became deafening. Dust and grit assaulted her eyes, forcing her to squeeze them shut and flow with the aimless direction of the crowd.

## 5

"Senator, turn on Channel Seven," said a familiar voice on the phone.

Without acknowledging the caller, Charles Ames hung up and punched the remote on his desk. Across the room a large-screen TV flickered to life: thousands of people on the lawn of the Federal Building. A young man threw flyers from a crane bucket with one hand while shooting lightning in the air with his other. *"When Jeff LaFayette's girlfriend was apprehended by LAPD detective Ralph Banner, the young man turned the laser gun on the policeman."*

Ames watched the detective fly into the crowd and pitch forward on his face. *"The moment LaFayette acted violently, Police Captain Daniel Grover ordered the crane operator to drop the basket."* The next shaky pictures from a handheld camera were of LaFayette, handcuffed, being thrown into a police car. *"LaFayette's girlfriend, Perrin McKinley, is being sought for questioning at this time. Anyone knowing her whereabouts is requested to call the Los Angeles Police Department."* The camera cut to a still close-up of Perrin.

*"This effort to stop Senator Charles Ames' solar-laser generator project began last night when LaFayette destroyed the capstone of the Beverly Hills . . ."* Ames lowered the TV volume and picked up the phone.

"Find out who LaFayette is and who's behind him. This kind of story will get international coverage."

Ames slammed the receiver back in its cradle and twisted his chair around to observe the ocean view from the window of his Pacific Palisades home. The dark sea was empty, its color blending with the storm-cloaked sky to conceal the horizon. The senator sat quietly, his jaw clenched, unconsciously rolling a gold pen back and forth in his hand.

\* \* \* \* \*

Marcus McKinley had already seen the newscast when Perrin reached her father on the phone. "Dad, don't ask me any questions. Just listen. I don't dare go back to our apartment, and I'm sure the police will be at your house soon. I need a good lawyer and fast."

"You've known Jerry McFarland all your life, Perrin. He's one of the best. But since it's Saturday I hope I can find him. Where are you now?"

"In a phone booth. I'm driving a rented car, so I don't think the police are on to it. I'll drive around and then call you in a half hour."

"Call my beeper. I'd better not be here when the police arrive."

It took two hours to find Jerry McFarland and set up a meeting at his Century City office. Perrin's father was waiting by the elevators in the underground parking facility as his daughter pulled to a stop in the nearly-empty garage.

She embraced him with a desperate hug that was interrupted by the opening elevator doors. They stepped in and Marcus McKinley pushed sixteen. His ebony hair had greyed becomingly at the temples, and his blue eyes matched his daughter's. Perrin had always believed the set of his chin suggested the stubbornness she'd inherited from him. He was a handsome, fifty-eight-year-old stock analyst with a tennis-court tan and a warm smile for his only daughter.

"In a dither?" he asked, squeezing her hand.

"Yeah," she said as they stepped off the elevator.

Jerry McFarland was sixty, with a thin face, a lean, wiry body and a tough demeanor. He'd cut short a golf game to meet with the McKinleys.

The mahogany-paneled law office seemed a peaceful refuge to Perrin. It took her nearly an hour to tell the whole story. A desktop TV was tuned to channel seven. When the station replayed the story as a "newsbreak," Jerry turned up the volume and watched closely.

"Past lives, mind-powered laser beams, conspiracy, good Lord," Jerry said, tilting back in his chair. "LAPD is the least of our problems. The government, the CIA, FBI, NSA . . . they're all going to want to stick pins in your boyfriend to find out what makes him tick. Then there's Senator Ames. He's powerful, he's mean, and he'll want the matter handled to serve his interests."

"What about Perrin's involvement?" Marcus asked.

"She didn't do anything but walk to the Federal Building with Jeff. But that may not stop the feds from putting her through the wringer. I was playing golf with a federal judge. I think I'll call him."

\* \* \* \* \*

"They won't charge Jeff until a lot of important people decide how they want the situation handled. That will be Sunday afternoon. The judge won't set bail until Monday morning," Jerry said as Marcus pulled his Lincoln Town Car into a metered parking place a half block from the West Los Angeles Police Station. Perrin sat in the front seat between the two men. "They'll hit Jeff with vandalism for destroying the capstone, but I doubt an assault charge will stick. Too many extenuating circumstances."

"Thank you for agreeing to represent Jeff, too," Perrin said.

"Hell, you'll probably get more publicity out of this case than anything you've ever handled," Marcus said and laughed.

"Just what I need," Jerry muttered. He patted Perrin's shoulder. "They've guaranteed there will be no charges filed based upon your involvement as you've related it to me," he said. "I'll be right there with you during the questioning."

As they approached the entrance, media personnel armed with

cameras and notebooks stepped from cars. The back doors of a Channel 11 van burst open and a man with a TV camera leaned into view.

"Miss McKinley! Miss McKinley, please take a moment to tell your side of the story," shouted a man waving a microphone. Flashes exploded in Perrin's eyes, momentarily blinding her.

"Can you zap people with crystals, too?" someone said.

"Hey, come on. The whole world wants to know about this."

Perrin looked from her father to Jerry McFarland, who shook his head. They pushed their way past the microphones, floodlights, and shouting people, up the stairs and into the front doors of the police department.

"This way please," said a man with narrow eyes and sharp, chiseled features. He wore a black suit and led the way. Perrin, her father and her lawyer followed a couple paces behind, down a sterile hallway, their footsteps echoing off the barren walls. Two men in suits followed until they entered a large office occupied by three more men.

"Which one of you is the lawyer?"

Jerry identified himself. The man in black pulled a wallet from his breast pocket and opened it to display White House credentials. "The US attorney general considers this to be a matter of the highest national security. The president is involved. Normal process of law is temporarily suspended. Jeff LaFayette and Perrin McKinley will leave immediately for Washington, DC.

Jerry raised his index finger, tapped the chest of the man in black, saying, "Just a minute. Nobody, including the president, is above the law."

"Come along, miss," said another man, grasping Perrin by the arm.

"Hold on," Marcus said, stepping forward to protect his daughter.

Letting go of Perrin's arm, the man threw a kidney punch into Marcus' side, sending him sprawling to the ground.

Perrin screamed.

While Jerry demanded his client's rights and Marcus writhed on the floor in agony, the federal agents dragged Perrin, struggling and screaming out the door, down a long hallway and into a car waiting by the back door of the police station.

\* \* \* \* \*

"If the public has any doubts about the solar-laser generator, activists will get involved, and we'll never get approval," Senator Ames said. The man he was addressing sat looking out the window of the Learjet 31 as it streaked through the night sky toward Washington, DC

"The activists have been on our side until now, Ames."

The senator motioned to the cabin steward and pointed to his empty drink glass. Moments later the steward served a fresh Glenmorangie on the rocks.

"I can't help it if some asshole comes out of the woodwork to denounce the project with carnival tricks," the senator said. His voice sounded tired.

"It wasn't a carnival trick that blew the capstone or flattened the cop. All they found on LaFayette was a simple quartz crystal."

"Who the hell could have set it up?" Ames asked, twisting his glass as he observed the pinpoint lights of Omaha, Nebraska, forty-seven thousand feet below.

"Someone who has something against you, Ames. That probably reduces the suspects to a few thousand." The senator didn't reply. The man continued. "We're talking about billions of dollars. If this goes haywire, you'll be left to explain."

"Crissake, they would tar and feather me," Ames said.

"For starters."

Ames lowered his voice. "I want LaFayette dead."

"That's easy."

* * * * *

The stretch limo with a privacy window between the driver and passengers pulled to a stop. Perrin, sitting between two men in the back seat, tensed as the man on her right opened the door and stepped out. Damp February air smelling of fuel oil wafted inside. A woman climbed into the car, grasped Perrin's right arm and snapped on a handcuff; the other cuff was secured to the woman's left wrist.

The privacy window lowered. "Everybody out," said the man in black.

Beside the car sat an Astra 1125 private jet. The woman tugged Perrin's arm and nodded at the stairs leading up into the plane. Perrin scanned the surroundings and decided they were at an airport near the ocean, and it wasn't LAX. She followed the woman up the stairs.

Onboard Jeff sat handcuffed to a man Perrin assumed to be another Federal agent. "JEFF, thank goodness!" Perrin jerked forward trying to reach him.

"Let them sit facing each other by the window," said the man in black. He nodded to one of his men, who reached into a briefcase and snapped on a recording device.

As they moved into the seating area, Perrin leaned down and kissed Jeff before they could stop her. "What did they do to you?" She nodded at a bruise swelling his eye and mottling the side of his face.

"When they dropped the bucket I landed on my face and dropped the crystal. Then a cop got in his licks with a nightstick. You okay?"

"My dad and our lawyer, Jerry McFarland, are involved. He'll represent you. Jerry contacted a federal judge before we even stepped into the West LA Police Station. But these clowns just moved in and took over." Perrin scanned the sour-looking group surrounding them.

"Don't sweat these guys," Jeff said, laughing. "I can make them disappear just by twitching my nose."

"Let's not push it, Jeff." Perrin looked at their jailers: two men, formally dressed, devoid of humor, and one middle-aged woman who looked like she'd swallowed a toad.

"The band and I always wanted to tour by private jet," Jeff said as the plane taxied down the runway, shooting into the night sky at 4,500 feet per minute. They leveled out at forty thousand feet.

"The guy you zapped at the Federal Building is going to be fine. They said the effect was that of an electrical stun gun."

"I could have told you that."

"They had your Prescott doctor on television by the time we were leaving McFarland's office. He was showing your X-rays and chattering like a true believer."

"I'll bet they even showed footage of my crumpled car in the creek bed."

She smiled, caressed him with her eyes.

"Perrin, remember when I was meditating this morning? I don't know much about meditation, but Odin does, and I'm learning fast. Anyway, I mentally went back to Atlantis, but it wasn't back in time, because time isn't what we think it is."

Perrin scowled at her lover, dipping her head toward their captors.
"Nah. Don't worry about these robots. They only understand orders from Der Führer."

The man beside him threw his elbow into Jeff's ribs, snarled, "Long-haired asshole!"

"Cutter, stuff it!" snapped the man in black.

Jeff puffed his cheeks and blew out slowly. "Honey, make a note. We turn Cutter into a blue cockroach." He shook his head and said, "Where was I? Oh yeah, I learned some real interesting stuff about time this morning. Several American physicists support the theory that time doesn't relate to reality. Research scientists have proven that a particle of energy can leave here and get there before it left. If this relates to humans, we may have died before we were born."

Perrin looked confused.

Jeff continued. "A lot of metaphysicians believe UFOs are from our future – our great-great grandchildren have developed a system of teleportation. In other words, all events that have ever been, are now, or ever will be, are eternally in existence; we as individuals simply move among these events. Maybe this explains precognitive dreams and psychic glimpses of the future. An analogy might be to imagine your experiences as beads strung on a thread that represents time. You are a small mark on the thread that strings the beads together, and you're being pulled through the beads, one at a time. The mark, which is you, is limited to experiencing each bead at a time, in sequence. Yet once in a while you get a glimpse of a bead to come and you experience a prophetic flash. If this is so then the major events in your life are pre-determined. But your reactions to the events are a matter of free will."

"You're getting too complicated for me," Perrin said. "If everything is happening now would this life be affecting your other lives?"

"Odin provided an example to help me understand. Think of all your lifetimes as a multilevel chess board. Each level of the board represents a lifetime. You have one chess piece on each level. Now think of each level as glass and look down upon it from above. It appears to be one chessboard. You see many individual figures, but they are all you – the kings, queens, knights, pawns – each is you in a different incarnation.

You in past lives, you in your present life, and you in future lives. Any move on any level has an effect upon the other levels—just as moving one chess piece in a chess game has an effect upon the total game."

Jeff took a deep breath and glanced at his captors. They were staring at him as if he were out of his mind. "All time is transpiring NOW," he continued. "Life is just a big multilevel chess game. Did you fellas get that on tape?"

"All time is an ever-present now," Perrin said, appearing to mull over the concept. She was looking out the window while actually observing the reflections of Cutter and the man in black sitting across the aisle. When they were both looking away, Perrin turned to Jeff, and raised her left hand to remove the backing to her crystal earring. She lowered her hand and rolled the small piece of silver between her thumb and index finger. Jeff winked.

"I have to go to the bathroom," Jeff said to Cutter. As he stood up he leaned over to kiss Perrin, stroked her face and palmed the two-inch quartz crystal.

## 6

"I'm going to tell you everything I know," Jerry McFarland said into the bank of microphones covering the podium of the Los Angeles Press Club. Marcus and Mary McKinley stood beside him on the stage. At 9 PM the room was jammed with reporters. On a riser along the back wall, eight television cameras focused on the speaker.

"Above all, ours is a nation of laws," McFarland shouted, stabbing the air with his index finger. "In our time we have ousted presidents who thought themselves above the law. Tonight, once again, representatives of our government have made a mockery of our judicial system."

McFarland used his most dramatic courtroom techniques to relate Jeff and Perrin's story. He detailed the events of the last twenty-four hours. He related the experiences at the police station and ended saying, "At this very minute Perrin McKinley and Jeff LaFayette have been robbed of their right to due process of law by the country's top cop, the attorney general of the United States of America. I'm asking for the free press of this country to make him account for his gestapo tactics."

Jerry turned to Marcus and Mary and whispered, "They'll circle Washington like sharks scenting blood."

\* \* \* \* \*

"How long until we get to Washington?" Jeff asked the man in the black suit.

"Ninety minutes."

Jeff looked at Perrin. "I'm going to try to take a nap."

She smiled. The lady agent handcuffed to Perrin scowled but didn't say anything.

Jeff closed his eyes, slipped his right hand into the pocket of his jeans and clasped the crystal earring. He mentally sent relaxing suggestions to his feet, lower legs, upper legs and then up through his body until all physical sensation faded away. His mind remained alert as he began to silently count down, visualizing himself falling through space, tumbling and twisting, then dropping like a felled bird out of a black sky. Number seven, deeper, deeper, deeper, down, down, down. Number six, deeper, deeper, deeper. . .

He counted down from seven to one five times before the black sky began to fade into midnight blue, then navy blue, and finally sky blue as he descended through billowing clouds toward a gleaming white city. He landed gently on his feet in a garden of fruit trees, ferns and rose bushes. A low wall enclosed the manicured courtyard. A fountain bubbled into the air, cascading water into a pool.

A man in his fifties, with shoulder-length black hair and copper-colored skin walked through an arch to welcome Jeff with a hearty embrace. "I didn't expect you again so soon."

"I don't have much time," Jeff said. "You talked before of astral projection—"

"You're in your astral body now."

"Can you help me project to someone else?"

"Of course. Capture their essence in your mind. Visualize how the person looks, how they move. Hear them speak. Say their name over and over, silently in your mind."

Jeff closed his eyes and imagined Senator Charles Ames. Images of Kesar and Ames overlapped and melted into each other until Jeff exerted his will to focus only on the image of the senator.

Odin's voice was far away, saying, "Now remain focused upon the mental image while you let your astral body slip away."

For a moment Jeff thought he'd awakened on the plane. But it was a different plane, with more luxurious appointments. Three men in the passenger section: a steward who sat in the rear and two men in the mid-section. One was Ames, the other had his faced turned, looking out the window.

They can't see me. They really can't see me, Jeff thought as he moved to within a few feet of the two men.

Ames' face was flushed, and he looked angry when he spoke. "The Yakata Eight wouldn't walk away clean if I told what I know about the Chancellor Project and your association with a Dutch industrialist and an East German munitions manufacturer."

"You are outliving your usefulness, Senator," the second man said, turning to Ames. Jeff recognized him immediately as Dr. Stanford Brandise, billionaire philanthropist and chairman of the Japanese-American Industrial Council.

"Let's just handle the situation," Ames said, as he tossed down a drink. "For five years the Japanese have been buying up the world's quartz crystals. Everything is in place. So take care of this LaFayette."

At the mention of his name, Jeff felt shock followed by a tugging at his arm. He resisted, then winced in pain as the handcuff cut into his wrist. He opened his eyes to see Perrin looking at him with loving concern. Cutter was twisting in his seat and a phone was ringing.

The man in black withdrew the phone from his breast pocket. He listened intently while looking directly into Jeff's eyes, then punched off the receiver without saying goodbye. He hit the intercom button. "Captain, we have a change of plans. Find a small, deserted airfield and set us down as soon as possible." There was a pause. "I don't care what you think. That's an order. And maintain radio silence."

"Why?" Jeff said loudly.

"You don't ask questions, Crystal Boy. You just go where I take you and it looks like it's going to be south eastern Ohio." He looked out the plane window, adjusting his shoulder holster while staring into the blackness.

Jeff glanced at Perrin. She was worried and he knew it. The plane dipped to the left and began to lose altitude.

"We aren't supposed to make it to Washington. Is that it?" Jeff asked quietly.

Cutter smiled sadistically at Jeff. The man in black didn't reply. The plane leveled out and the only sound in the cabin was the deep-throated roar of the jet engines. Minutes later the plane circled and dropped lower. From his window Jeff observed the moonlit, snow-covered terrain a thousand feet below. Occasional farm lights were the only signs of civilization.

Perrin laid her hand on Jeff's knee until the woman jerked her back. "What am I going to do with both of us handcuffed like animals?"

"Don't touch him again."

The intercom buzzed. The man in black picked it up. "It will do," he said. "When we land you're both to remain in the cockpit until I tell you differently. Understand?" There was a pause. "That's an order."

The landing was smooth, but the Astra 1125 began to slide sideways on the snow-slick runway. Jeff and Perrin held their breath as the pilot made his corrections and the plane straightened out and eased to a stop.

"Outside." The man in black threw open the hatch door.

Cutter jerked Jeff to his feet and into the aisle. The man in black was the first one down the stairway into the sub-zero white night. Jeff, still wearing his herringbone sport coat, shivered as he stepped into the wind. Halfway down the runway was a small tower on top of a café, and beyond the tower, two hangars. There were no lights. Jeff and Perrin were directed towards the tail of the plane.

"Uncuff them," said the man in black, drawing a large-frame automatic from under his arm. Cutter and the woman quickly followed orders, then joined their boss facing Jeff and Perrin.

"Oh, God, they're going to kill us!" Perrin screamed, grabbing Jeff's left arm.

"Why?" Jeff asked, drawing the already pulsating crystal from his pocket. The man in black was raising his handgun as Jeff raised the crystal and sent a burst of blue light sizzling out the tip. The light hit him in the chest, spinning him off his feet and into the snow. Cutter was drawing his weapon when the second burst of light hit him like a giant fist, doubling him over. He staggered for a moment like a drunk before pitching face first into the runway. The man in black pulled himself up on one elbow to search for his handgun, which was already in Jeff's hand. The woman ran for the plane.

"Stop her!" Jeff yelled as Perrin jumped forward, darting toward the stairway. The woman was on the fifth step when Perrin dove for her foot, grabbed it and yanked hard, dropping the woman face down onto the stairs. Holding onto the foot, Perrin struggled to her feet and dragged the woman, her face bouncing down the steel stairs and into the snow. Perrin was trying to decide what to do next when she felt Jeff's hand on her arm.

"Back in the plane. Now." He pushed her up the stairway in front of him. Once inside, he threw the hatch closed and moved quickly to the cockpit door, opening it with a jerk. "Gentlemen, it's time to leave." He brandished the man in black's handgun.

"You don't need that," the captain replied. "We saw what happened. They would have killed us after killing you."

The jets roared to life. The plane taxied a little farther down the snow-packed runway before turning. Without hesitating, it shot forward, past the three stunned figures in the snow, and catapulted into the night sky.

"Somebody high on the power scale wants you dead," the co-pilot said to Jeff, still hunched in the doorway.

"We'll leave you out of it. Just tell them we forced you to fly us out of there."

"They'll break into that airport building and call Washington," the captain said. "Other planes will be on our tail within twenty minutes."

"Where can you put us down?" Jeff said.

"Clarksburg, West Virginia, in fifteen minutes."

"How far is it from Washington?" Jeff asked.

"About two hundred miles."

"Do it," Jeff said, looking over his shoulder at Perrin, her face ashen, her body trembling.

\* \* \* \* \*

The message on the answering machine filled Marcus McKinley with more fear than he already felt, as if that were possible. Perrin's voice was shaky as she said, "Dad, I'm all right. Please tell Jerry McFarland that the people who kidnapped us tried to kill us. Thanks to Jeff's ability we got away. Tell him Ames and his partner Dr. Stanford Brandise are behind it. The two of them are partners with something called the Yata—" There was a pause in the message while Marcus heard Perrin conferring with Jeff on the pronunciation. "They're partners with the Yakata Eight on the solar-laser amplification project. Also have Jerry check Brandise's association with a Dutch industrialist and a German munitions manufacturer on the Chancellor Project. Then tell the world that Jeff and I will demonstrate at the Washington Monument Monday at noon."

Marcus picked up the phone, punched Jerry McFarland's number and placed the receiver to his ear. The phone was dead, and someone was knocking on the front door.

* * * * *

"We'll stop them before they get to Washington," said the man in black to Senator Charles Ames. They were sitting in the study of the senator's Washington, DC home.

"That's a confident statement from somebody that couldn't neutralize two handcuffed civilians," Ames snarled in response. He was shaking his head as he stood up and walked slowly to the window. The Sunday morning pre-dawn light silhouetted the naked trees lining the snow-covered ridge behind the house.

* * * * *

Driving a stolen Ford Tempo, Jeff and Perrin pulled into a roadside diner on the western edge of Pittsburgh, Pennsylvania, at 8 AM.

"Two black coffees and two orders of hotcakes," Perrin said to the tired-eyed counter man.

"He looks worse than we do," Jeff whispered to his lover.

"I got a couple hours' sleep while you drove," she said. "I feel pretty good."

"How much money do you have?" Jeff asked.

Perrin checked her purse. "Thirty-six dollars and change.

Plus Visa, American Express, and my checkbook."

"They'll be monitoring credit cards," Jeff said. "They took my wallet when they booked me. It's not much."

"And we need a crystal, Jeff. I'm going to check the Yellow Pages."

Perrin flipped through a phone book that hung on a wire beneath a dial phone on the wall. Jeff sipped his coffee and tried to brush away the mental cobwebs of exhaustion. He couldn't focus on anything beyond his immediate environment. Fifties diners were a current fad, but this was a worn-out original and looked twice its age. A grey-haired man in bib overalls sat three stools away, his lunchbox at his feet. At the other end of the counter a young black man wearing earphones bobbed up and down to an unheard beat.

"The Crown Chakra opens at ten," Perrin said, swinging onto the counter stool. "They're sure to have crystals."

Following breakfast, Jeff and Perrin used the café bathrooms to clean up as best they could. By 9:30 AM they were sitting in the Ford Tempo across the street from the metaphysical bookstore. It was located on the edge of downtown in a graceless turn-of-the-century brick building. In the window were displays of New Age books and tapes. Faceted crystal balls hung on strings in the window, slowly turning, flashing in the reflected sunlight bathing the front of the building. The slushy street was deserted.

"I wonder how many people are hunting us?" Perrin said, cuddling into Jeff for warmth and mental support. The car motor was running with the heater on, but she was still chilled. Her racing jacket wasn't intended for eastern winter wear.

"The government thinks we're threats to national security. Ames knows we're a threat to him. I'd guess every police agency in the country is on our tail, plus maybe the National Guard and the Boy Scouts."

She punched him playfully in the ribs as they watched a bearded young man in round glasses, a stocking cap, a Navy pea coat and jeans walk down the street toward their car. He cut across the street before reaching them, and walked up the steps to the Crown Chakra. A moment later he was inside and lights snapped on.

"Come on," Jeff said getting out of the car. They darted across the street and up the steps. The door was unlocked and they entered the store.

The smell of incense permeated the interior.

The shopkeeper had taken off his coat and was wearing a plaid flannel shirt. Tall with a little potbelly, he had a red and bushy beard. Perrin thought he looked like a fat pencil.

"Morning," Jeff said. "Do you have any crystals?"

The young man smiled. Perrin thought she caught a flash of recognition. "Over here." He gestured toward a large display under the side window. "I'm Harvey Tanner," he said, offering Jeff his hand.

"Jeff LaFayette," he responded without thinking.

"I know," Harvey said. "Did you really blow the top off the Beverly Hills City Hall with a quartz crystal?"

Jeff and Perrin stiffened. "How did you . . . ?"

"How? Good Lord. According to the news, you two are the biggest desperadoes since Bonnie and Clyde. They're flashing your pictures on the TV every thirty minutes. The car you're driving was the only one stolen in Clarksburg after your arrival there last night, so they're even showing pictures of it." Harvey pointed out the window at the Tempo parked across the street.

"Please believe us, we didn't—"

"Hey," Harvey interrupted. "Yesterday, when I watched the interview with your Arizona doctor telling about your 'Atlantis delusions,' I understood."

"You did?" Perrin said. "I wish to hell I did."

"You're using your Atlantean knowledge. You're trying to warn the world that what happened on the lost continent could happen again."

Jeff looked at Harvey, stunned.

"We've got to find the right crystal and get to Washington," Perrin said, an edge of desperation in her voice.

Harvey responded with a deep, honest laugh and a smile that seemed to light up from within. He knelt down, opened a drawer beneath the crystal display and took out a long wooden box. Jeff looked from Harvey to the box and carefully opened it. Inside was a foot-long jade rod carved to look like a plumed rattlesnake. Emerging from the snake's mouth was a perfect eight-inch quartz crystal.

Jeff trembled in subconscious recognition.

"Atlantean," Harvey said. "The style that was passed on to the

Atlantean Mesoamerican settlements—the Mayans, the Toltecs and the people of Teotihuacan."

Jeff slowly lifted the rod from its black velvet bed and held it to the center of his forehead.

"It's yours," Harvey said. "I've always known it was meant for a special purpose."

"I don't have the money to pay you now, but I—"

Harvey interrupted Jeff. "You can pay me by letting me help you."

"Help us?" Perrin said in disbelief.

"Yes. And we'll start by ditching that car you're driving far away from here or they'll make the connection to me."

"But your store," Perrin said. "You can't—"

"Sure I can. I'll leave a note on the door. My customers will understand. I'm closed Mondays, so I can drive you to Washington tomorrow morning."

After leaving the car on a back street, Jeff and Perrin rode in Harvey's 1969 Volkswagen van back to his apartment a few blocks from the bookstore. It was a two-bedroom on the third floor of an old brownstone. Hanging from the center of the high-ceilinged living room was a large pyramid. Visionary art lined the walls and a backlighted crystal display glowed from a glass case that hung on the wall above the couch. One bedroom served as a warehouse for metaphysical books and products for the store.

"Sleep now," Harvey said. "I'll take care of business, line up some fresh clothes for you, and be back by dinner time."

Perrin showered while Jeff relaxed in front of the TV. Andre Agassi was playing Boris Becker on a palm-lined tennis court. He channel-surfed past MTV, Bugs Bunny, and a couple of fundamentalist preachers, until he found CNN. He almost jumped when his picture appeared on the screen.

"... *after forcing the plane to land at this remote Ohio airfield, Jeff LaFayette used his uncanny crystal ability to sadistically punish the two male agents, while his girlfriend Perrin McKinley mercilessly beat the female agent.*" The camera cut to an extreme close-up of the woman's bloodied face. After a report of the incidents in Beverly Hills and at the Federal Building, a reporter standing in front of the Clarksburg airport building appeared on the screen, microphone in hand. "*A reward of one hundred thousand dollars is being offered for information leading to the capture and . . .*"

Jeff snapped off the set and sat frozen, wondering about Harvey. He opened the box containing the jade and crystal rod, looked at it, closed the top, opened it again. Trust, he thought. Trust.

The bedroom was black as a cave when a noise pulled Jeff out of a deep sleep and away from his Atlantean teleportation lesson. Perrin was cuddled into his back, still breathing deeply. Jeff groped in the darkness for the jade rod. He couldn't remember if he'd left it under the pillow or on the bedside table. He'd thought of both places prior to falling asleep. Before he could find the rod the door opened and a man stood silhouetted in light from the living room.

"Jeff, Perrin. It's time to wake up," Harvey said. "It's eight o'clock. Dinner's ready."

"You're a lifesaver, Harvey," Jeff said, eating his second vegeburger. "If these aren't meat, what are they?"

"Soybeans, vegetables and herbal flavorings," Harvey said proudly.

Jeff raised his eyebrows and looked at the burger in his hands. Perrin smiled.

"The feds came to visit me this afternoon. Showed me your pictures and asked if you'd been in to buy any crystals."

"Did they tell you about the reward?" Jeff asked.

Harvey smiled. "A million dollars wouldn't tempt someone who accepts karma as their basis of reality."

The TV news was playing in the background. Twenty minutes into the meal, the LaFayette/McKinley story was replayed but there was no mention of the planned Washington Monument demonstration.

"If Jerry McFarland got my message the press would have that information," Perrin said. "What have they done to my father?" Tears trembled on the edges of her eyelids. Jeff reached across the table, squeezed her hand.

The fear quickly turned to anger, as she set her jaw and said, "A call from here might be traced directly back to us. But I could ask one of the women I work with at the studio to go to a phone booth and call Jerry, the *Los Angeles Times,* the *Washington Post,* and a few odd TV stations."

\* \* \* \* \*

Jeff, Perrin and Harvey were listening to news radio when they arrived in Washington DC at 11:30 AM Monday morning in the Volkswagen van. For the third time they heard the announcer say, *"The senator's solar-laser generator is an experimental concept in which the rays of the sun are focused and amplified into a bank of huge quartz crystals. Until now this privately funded project has been praised by the California State Legislature and environmentalists alike. According to Senator Ames it offers the safe, clean energy alternative our country needs so badly.*

*"The financial sponsor of the project is a corporation called California LazerTec. But acting upon a tip from Perrin McKinley's lawyer, when we attempted to investigate this corporation, we found it to be funded by private philanthropic organizations that were funded by other philanthropic organizations in a circle that seems to have no end. In other words, the people behind CLT don't seem to want us to know who they are. However, we are also investigating a connection to Dr. Stanford Brandise and the Yakata Eight, a Japanese conglomerate that is not allowed to do business in the United States.*

*"If Senator Ames has conspired with the Yakata Eight he will have a great deal to answer for. Dr. Brandise is out of the country and could not be reached for comment.*

*"According to unconfirmed reports, Jeff LaFayette and Perrin McKinley plan a noon demonstration at the Washington Monument."*

Harvey turned down the volume. "You realize even if you win, you lose," he said. "They'll never leave you alone. Even if the feds back off, the scientists of the world will want to dissect your brain."

"I know," Jeff said. He noticed the horrified look on Perrin's face. "But right now we'd better get to the Washington Monument. It's show time."

Light snow was falling and the Washington streets were more congested than usual because traffic was being routed away from the Washington Monument. Harvey had borrowed a sweater and warmer coat for Perrin. He'd given Jeff his winter topcoat which was about six inches too long.

"I don't know how we'll ever be able to repay you, Harvey," Perrin said, squeezing his shoulder.

"Hell, you're letting me help you save the world," Harvey replied. "Good karma, you know."

They were several blocks from the Washington Monument when Jeff directed Harvey to stop the car at the corner. "Harvey, thank you for everything." Jeff offered his hand. "When Perrin and I get out of the van, I'll use the crystal to generate a protective force field around us. It should protect us from anything, but I've never done it before. I'd suggest you watch from a distance."

Harvey nodded, mumbled, "Good luck."

Jeff opened the door, and stepped out into the crowded street. Perrin followed and took his left hand. With his right holding the jade and crystal rod, Jeff closed his eyes and focused a protective aura. The quartz crystal glowed and hummed as a blue light emerged from the tip to form a ball of shimmering, translucent blue light around the couple.

Perrin turned to see Harvey still sitting behind the wheel of his van, his eyes wide, his mouth open. "We'll be back to visit you in Pittsburgh, Harvey. I promise."

"Let's go," Jeff said, gently tugging at her hand.

The first people who noticed them just stared. Then someone screamed and the commotion started. Some were running away from them, others toward them. "What's weird about a man and a woman walking down the street inside a big blue force field?" Jeff said, laughing.

The people who tried to reach them bounced off the force field as if it were a plate glass window. A businessman in a suit stood to the side and rubbed his injured head. Everyone was yelling at once.

"What ya gonna do?" screeched an old woman.

"Zap the president while you're at it," yelled a middle-aged blue-collar laborer.

"Come on, man, let me in there with ya," said a black kid on a bicycle.

At the corner a policeman appeared and stood, legs spread and planted firmly on the sidewalk in front of the couple. "Jeff LaFayette and Perrin McKinley, you're under arrest!" he shouted.

Jeff and Perrin continued to walk towards him. He put up his hand to touch the force field and was forced back as the couple inched forward. "Stop, damn it," he shouted again, drawing his nightstick from his belt. When the couple continued walking the policeman swung the baton at the shimmering ball of light.

The shock of hitting the force field stung the cop's hand so badly he dropped the baton, which was instantly picked up by the kid on the bicycle who sped away with his prize.

Across the street from the Mall and the walkway leading to the Washington Monument, a dozen police officers and hundreds of screaming, pushing people surrounded them, forcing a slowed pace to avoid crushing others as they forced their way through the throng. A truck with a TV unit on top was parked by the curb. In an effort to protect the population, the police helped to shove people out of their path. As they crossed the street, Jeff and Perrin saw a line of patrol cars forming a wall blocking the entrance to the Mall.

The police directed the couple between an opening in the cars and allowed them to enter the expanse leading to the monument. Swirling blue and red lights swept the scene, reflecting in the luminous force field. Squawking radios drowned out the sounds of the crowd. A dozen manned TV cameras were in place. Two hundred yards ahead stood a group of people. Beyond them was the Washington Monument, a gleaming, white marble obelisk, 555 feet high, topped with a solid aluminum capstone.

Perrin was trembling so violently she leaned on Jeff for support.

"This way," said a policeman, as he walked to the left of the force field, guiding them down the Mall toward the group of people. At one hundred yards, Perrin realized that her mother, father and Jerry McFarland were standing with police, soldiers and other government employees dressed in suits and wearing topcoats. Her mother waved. Perrin waved and blew a kiss.

Jerry McFarland, accompanied by men on his left and right, stepped forward and walked to within five feet of the force field. "Perrin, Jeff, I'm glad you're all right." Jerry gestured toward the tall, grey-haired man on his right. "This is Robert Wellington, the attorney general of the United States. And the gentleman on my left is federal justice Thornton Blackstone."

The attorney general spoke. "I have to ask you to give yourselves up. We are already investigating the connections between Senator Ames and Dr. Brandise. At this time you're only guilty of destroying Beverly Hills property. And we have some questions about your encounter on the plane from Los Angeles."

Perrin interrupted. "Your agents were on that plane. Someone called them and ordered us murdered."

"If that's what happened, we'll find out," the attorney general said.

"We've been in custody once. Not again, thank you," Jeff replied.

"You don't have much choice, young man. The Mall is surrounded by a force that will easily penetrate that light bubble."

"Please," the judge said to Jeff and Perrin. "I'll personally guarantee your safety and force an investigation."

"Justice Blackstone, Mr. Attorney General, Mr. McFarland, be realistic. We have no intention of surrendering, for rather obvious reasons. I want access to the TV networks at the entrance to the Mall."

"Absolutely not," replied the attorney general.

Jeff locked eyes with Robert Wellington as he raised the throbbing crystal rod toward the capstone of the Washington Monument. "I want to say a few words, then we'll leave peacefully," Jeff said softly.

The attorney general raised his right hand and rows of battle-clad policemen appeared. An armored vehicle roared into the Mall and advanced to within twenty yards of the force field. The three men began to back away.

Perrin called out to Jerry McFarland. "Are my mom and dad okay?"

Jerry sputtered, "Yes-s-s."

"Tell them Jeff and I will be back to visit soon."

Jeff aimed the crystal at the monument capstone and willed the crackling beam of energy to fire into the air as sizzling blue lightning. The sound echoed through the Mall like hissing electrical static. The three men turned and began to run. The attorney general stumbled, fell, stood up and turned to scream, "FIRE!"

From all sides guns roared and bullets ricocheted off the force field. The armored vehicle grabbed for traction as it lurched forward, running full speed at the force field. It rammed the shimmering ball of light with a crumpling thud that caved in the front of the vehicle and released a stream of whining radiator steam.

As Jeff held the crystal rod steady the Washington Monument capstone began to melt, dribbling like frosting down the sides of the monument.

"Attack!" someone ordered, and an army of men assaulted the force field. Jeff lowered his arm and smiled at the crazed faces of the attacking policemen. When they eventually realized the futility of their efforts they backed away, dismayed.

Jeff and Perrin turned and walked back to the Mall entrance and the television cameras.

"Does someone have a microphone that can be heard by everyone here?" Jeff called out.

A young woman quickly ran a cordless microphone to within a foot of the force field, laid it on the ground and returned to her position behind a camera. Jeff reached through the field, picked it up and held it to his lips as the cameras zoomed in on the couple. Behind them the now flat-topped monument glistened in the winter sun.

"I apologize for destroying public property, but it was the only way to make you listen," Jeff said. "What you have just seen is a minor demonstration of the power of the human mind directed through a crystal amplifier. This was a common ability on the lost continent of Atlantis, where I lived another life 28,000 years ago, as you perceive time. The concept of reincarnation is real.

"My initial demonstration in Beverly Hills was to draw attention to the Solar-Laser Amplification Power Project planned for the San Joaquin Valley. The danger of such a project far exceeds that of the nuclear power plants you already fear. Solar-laser amplification destroyed Atlantis, and it could destroy the United States if you allow it to be developed.

"Stop all solar-laser explorations and stop the other destructive practices that are devastating our world. We must stop polluting the air and the groundwater, stop the ozone depletion, and resolve the hazardous waste and acid rain problems. None of this will happen unless you get involved. Do your part and demand that our government act.

"George Washington said, 'Our cause is noble, it is the cause of mankind!' Surely the most noble cause is to save this planet. Get involved."

Jeff turned away from the cameras to face the Washington Monument. He aimed the crystal at the obelisk and a burst of blue energy shot from the tip of the crystal and exploded into the marble.

Chips flew into the air, scattering like glistening rain over the mall as the laser beam cut giant letters down the face of the monument, forming the words,

G
E
T

I
N
V
O
L
V
E
D

When it was done, Jeff took Perrin in his arms and kissed her tenderly. "I always wanted to play to a huge audience," he whispered. "And here it finally happens and I don't even have my guitar." As the TV cameras zoomed in for a close-up, the lovers began to fade away. At first, it was as if a fog had manifested within the force field, but it soon became apparent that they were disappearing.

When Perrin opened her eyes she was descending from billowing clouds toward a gleaming white city. There were more parks than housing areas. She counted, one, two, then three open-air amphitheaters. There were trains, hovering discs, moving sidewalks. She couldn't believe her eyes.

"Teleportation. The only way to fly," Jeff said, as they landed gently in a garden of fruit trees, ferns and rose bushes. A white wall enclosed a manicured courtyard, a bubbling fountain and a reflective pool.

Hand-in-hand, they walked through the garden, past the rose bushes, into their new home.

# About The Author

**Dick Sutphen** (pronounced Sut-fen) has written several of the all-time bestselling books on metaphysics and reincarnation, including seven titles for Simon and Schuster Pocket Books, who calls him "America's foremost psychic researcher." *You Were Born Again to Be Together* has sold nearly a million copies. Other recent titles include: *Finding Your Answers Within, Earthly Purpose, The Oracle Within, Reinventing Yourself, Radical Spirituality* and *The Spiritual Path Guidebook. Heart Magic* is a collection of Dick's mystical fiction about finding love and answers.

Over 125,000 people have attended a Sutphen Seminar, which are conducted every year in major U.S. cities and around the world. The "5-Day Professional Past-Life Therapy Training" and "Metaphysical Counselor Training" teach people to hypnotize, regress and counsel others. Dick has also created over 200 audio and video mind-programming tapes and CDs now in world-wide release. He lives with his wife Tara and their children in Malibu, California.

# FREE MAGAZINE

Dick and Tara Sutphen publish a quarterly magazine that is mailed to 100,000+ book/tape buyers and seminar attendees. A sample issue is free, and if you purchase a product or attend a seminar, you will receive the publication free for two years. If you purchased this book in a bookstore, send us the receipt (or a copy) and we'll add you to the mailing list for two years.

Each issue is approximately 76 pages and contains news, research reports and articles on metaphysics, psychic exploration and self-help, in addition to providing information on Sutphen Seminars, and 300 audio and video tapes: hypnosis, meditation, sleep programming, subliminal programming, and inner-harmony music.

**Valley of the Sun Publishing**
**Box 38, Malibu, CA 90265**

135

# Books From Valley of the Sun

☐ **New Age Short Stories** By Dick Sutphen ................................ B942 – $10.00
☐ **Radical Spirituality** By Dick Sutphen ............................... B938 – $12.95
☐ **Metaphysical Techniques That Really Work**
By Audrey Craft Davis ........................................................... B939 – $12.95
☐ **Predestined Love** By Dick Sutphen .............................. B940 – $14.95
☐ **How To Absolutely, Positively**
**Look 5 to 10 Years Younger** By Sharon Boyd ....................... B937 – $12.00
☐ **How To Believe In Nothing & Set Yourself Free**
By Michael Misita .................................................................. B936 – $9.98
☐ **The Soulmate Process** By Bob Lancer ............................. B928 – $9.98
☐ **The Spiritual Path Guidebook** By Dick Sutphen ............. B930 – $5.95
☐ **Simple Solutions** By Dick Sutphen ................................ B941 – $5.95
☐ **Reinventing Yourself** By Dick Sutphen ......................... B927 – $9.98
☐ **Blame It On Your Past Lives** By Tara Sutphen ................ B933 – $9.98
☐ **Yoga, Youth & Reincarnation** By Jess Stearn .................. B935 – $9.98
☐ **SEDONA: Psychic Energy Vortexes** ............................... B922 – $9.98
☐ **Heart Magic** By Dick Sutphen ....................................... B926 – $9.98
☐ **The Nasty Dragon Who Became A Nice Puppy** (*reincarnation for children*)
Book and tape by Dick Sutphen ............................................ B929 – $10.98
☐ **Past-Life Therapy In Action**
By Dick Sutphen & Lauren L. Taylor ...................................... B915 – $7.95
☐ **Enlightenment Transcripts** By Dick Sutphen .................. B923 – $3.95
☐ **The Star Rover** By Jack London ..................................... B914 – $8.95
☐ **Assertiveness Training** By Dick Sutphen ....................... B980 – $3.95
☐ **A Veil Too Thin** By Betty Riley ...................................... B920 – $2.95
☐ **Tape Instruction & Idea Manual** ................................... B912 – $2.95

## • From Simon & Schuster Pocket Books •

☐ **You Were Born Again to Be Together**
By Dick Sutphen ..................................................................... B904 – $6.99
☐ **Past Lives, Future Loves** By Dick Sutphen ..................... B905 – $5.50
☐ **Earthly Purpose** By Dick Sutphen .................................. B908 – $4.95
☐ **FindingYour Answers Within** By Dick Sutphen ............... B907 – $5.99

These titles may be purchased at your local metaphysical store, or directly from Valley of the Sun. Credit card orders, call 1-800-421-6603. By mail, send checks or credit card information to **Valley of the Sun, Box 38, Malibu, CA 90265.** Include $3.50 per order for shipping.